Acclaim for **ANDRE DUBUS I**

THE CAGE KEEPER

"Touching and real. . . . Insightful. . . . Dubus masterfully captures the psychology of abuse." —*San Francisco Chronicle*

"Powerful. . . . [Dubus has] a keen eye for observing people on the edge." —*The Boston Herald*

"Dubus has a fine ear, terse syntax, and the discipline to write some very fine stories." —*Interview*

"Jolt[s] readers into contemplating the nature of evil. . . . This author takes risks [and they] pay off." —*Library Journal*

"Dubus displays a firm grasp of the requirements of satisfying short fiction and a wide-ranging eye tightly focused on the telling detail. . . . No unessential information diminishes the impact of these stories, but what does matter—to both characters and readers—is grippingly and generously portrayed." —*Publishers Weekly*

"A wondrous debut by a fresh and bold young writer. But Andre Dubus III writes with the wisdom of age: sorrow and compassion are the marrow of these tough, delicate, utterly human stories."
—Susan Dodd,
author of *No Earthly Notion* and *Mamaw*

ANDRE DUBUS III

THE CAGE KEEPER

Andre Dubus III is the author of two other books, the novels *House of Sand and Fog* and *Bluesman*. *House of Sand and Fog* was a finalist for the National Book Award, the *Los Angeles Times* Book Prize, and the L. L. Winship/PEN New England Award, a selection of the Oprah Book Club, and an American Library Association Notable Book. Dubus has been awarded a Guggenheim Fellowship, a Pushcart Prize for his essay "Tracks and Ties," and a National Magazine Award for Fiction for his story "Forky," which is included in *The Cage Keeper*. His work has appeared in *The Best Spiritual Writing 1999* and *The Best American Essays 1994*. In 1994 Dubus was one of three finalists for the Prix de Rome given by the American Academy and Institute of Arts and Letters. He lives in Newburyport, Massachusetts, with his wife and three children.

Also by **ANDRE DUBUS III**

Bluesman

House of Sand and Fog

THE CAGE KEEPER

THE CAGE KEEPER

& Other Stories

ANDRE DUBUS III

VINTAGE CONTEMPORARIES
Vintage Books
A Division of Random House, Inc.
New York

FIRST VINTAGE CONTEMPORARIES EDITION, OCTOBER 2001

The stories included here have been revised slightly since first published in book form.

Library of Congress Cataloging-in-Publication Data
Dubus, Andre, 1959–
The cage keeper and other stories / Andre Dubus III.
p.   cm.
ISBN 0-375-72774-4
I. Title
PS3554.U2652C34 1989b
813'.54—dc20 89-1213
CIP

Book design by Mia Risberg

www.vintagebooks.com

Printed in the United States of America
10   9   8   7   6   5   4

For my mother, Patricia Lowe Dubus,
and for my father, Andre Dubus.

CONTENTS

THE CAGE KEEPER

THE CAGE KEEPER

For Mac

It's midnight in December, an hour past lights out, and I'm walking the hall of the women's wing. I open the doors fast so the hinges don't squeak and I run the beam of my flashlight over the beds. I try not to shine it in anybody's face while they're sleeping but sometimes I have to if their hair is in the way or something. They don't like that. Emma, this black woman from the projects of east Denver, she's mean; once I shined the light in her eyes and she threw her clock radio at me, yelled something like, "Get that damn light outta my *face*." I had to put her on restriction and cancel four of her weekend furloughs for that. Emma has ten kids and I guess I'm supposed to feel sorry for her when she can't get back to Denver to see them after throwing a radio at me. Fact is, I'm not too popular around here anyway. Leon is, though.

Leon's black and he lifts weights down at a gym near the university here in Boulder. His father's a realtor like mine, so he didn't grow up poor. And he doesn't let any of the black inmates come across with their "Hey, brother" malarkey either. Usually, when they start a sentence like that with him, they're trying to butter him up for some favor or another and Leon knows it. But he just puts his finger to their chest lightly and says, "Don't be giving me no brother shit, Clay. Now go wash down the mess hall walls." But he is more popular than I am. Not that I'm very worried about it, because I'm not. Like my older brother, Mark, the House Director, said to us in a meeting once: "If the inmates like you too much, then you're not doing your job properly." Leon does his job; it's just that he looks at these people differently than I do. We talked about this over a couple beers at The Rhino once after our four P.M. to one A.M. shift. He said that it's probably because he's black that he roots for the underdog. Me. I don't look at it that way; I don't believe that all convicted adult felons are underdogs. Plus, I have always felt for the person who just had their car stolen, or was mugged or raped or even killed. Those are the ones I feel sorry for. And I guess even though Leon and I approach our jobs in pretty much the same way, which is rule enforcer first, someone to talk to second, the inmates must pick up on this philosophical difference somehow.

It's amazing how they can do that. Like the last time we came out of a staff meeting after having just decided to initiate a surprise room-to-room search for contraband. When we got upstairs most everybody was in their rooms organizing things, cleaning up, and I'm sure, tossing an item or two out the window into the alley.

Leon says somebody had to have listened in on us, though if they're caught doing that they could lose their privileges for a month, but I don't think so. I'm beginning to think they can just pick up on these things; the way certain kinds of animals can smell a human a long way off in the distance, they feel us coming with our contraband-evidence bags, our Scotch tape, and red ball-point pens.

I finish checking the west end of the women's wing, close the door to Paulina's room, then mark a check beside her name on my clipboard. I walk down the hall and with the red plastic end of my flashlight, I knock once on Maggie Nickerson's door. I go in then shine the light down at the base of her bed. Her old face is sunk into the soft part of the pillow and her blue sleeping cap is pulled tightly over her scalp. There is gray in the auburn hair at her temples. When I first started working here, I thought she was a cleaning lady or something. I didn't know then that all the inmates did the cleaning themselves. Every time I saw her she had a mop or a broom or a dustcloth in her hand. Around the first or second week of November I asked her how a young single guy like me was going to cook a turkey by himself. She didn't say anything at the time, just kind of smiled like she hadn't understood the question. Two days before Thanksgiving she came down to the office and handed me a white index card with directions on one side on how to roast a turkey. On the other side she had written: "To Allen, a nice young man with nobody to cook for him yet. Your Friend, Maggie." A week later I read her file. Five years ago, on an August night in a trailer park near Longmont, she shot her drunk husband three times in the face with his own gun, a .38 snub-nosed revolver. They were sitting at the kitchen table at the time. One bullet is supposed to have entered his right eye and exited the back of his head hitting their nineteen-year-old daughter, Angela, in the knee. I've met her. She's very slender, almost frail-looking, with narrow hips and big breasts, and her face always looks like it's about to tell you bad news. But her hair is black and her eyes are dark and she is very pretty. I shine my light near the bedside table and see the papier-mâché Christmas tree that Angela and her little boy made for Maggie. It's painted dark green with little white Styrofoam crystals glued all over it. On top is a red star made out of construction paper. I look once more at Maggie's blue sleeping cap, mark her name off on my clipboard, then flick off my flashlight and pull the door shut.

On the second floor, I stop and look out the big window that faces the street. The night sky is so pretty out here. There are no city lights like in Denver where I live, and you can see the quarter moon so clearly hanging there bright above the sheer rise of Dead Goat Ridge. Below it, in the middle of one of the steepest-looking foothills, is a huge glowing five-pointed star nestled in the snow and pine trees. Leon tells me there's a fancy French restaurant up there and what you see that looks magical but isn't, is a huge wooden frame built about six feet off the ground in the shape of a star, a string of three-hundred-watt light bulbs nailed all around it. He says some Christmases a couple of the valets from the restaurant have to go up there in snowshoes and dig it out when the snow gets too deep. I look away from the star down to the snow- and ice-covered roofs of fraternity row, then down farther to the street corner in front of the center. There's a cruiser from the Boulder County Sheriff's Department parked just out of the circle of light the streetlamp gives off. A flame lights a cigarette on the driver's side. I think about what that state trooper said before he left tonight. Leon and I had just given him a copy of our escape report on Elroy and he was leaving in a hurry, but not before he turned to us and said, "Don't take this lightly now. We're talking about a convicted murderer here." Then he tipped his visor with two fingers like John Wayne and said, "Stay away from those windows" and left. None of the officers from the sheriff's department would have talked down to us like that; they know what a good program this is. I think it's us not wearing uniforms or carrying weapons that the troopers don't understand. Ten years ago these rooms were full of sorority girls, and we're still right in the middle of fraternity row. There are no bars on the windows. If one of our fifty-two inmates wants to leave, we're not going to stop him. Not many leave though. All of them are looking at parole. And if they do escape, they can expect another four to eight years' hard time tacked onto their original sentence. That's why I can't figure Elroy doing what he did tonight, though the signs were definitely there.

These past few nights he has been coming down to the staff office just to talk with Leon and me. Well, we got a big kick out of that one, Elroy wanting to talk to *us*. Lately, he has been submitting essays to the house paper about Big Brother and the Police State we're all living in and the so-called merits of anarchy. In one of them he referred to us correctional technicians as "ball-licking lackeys for Ronald Reagan's Ministry of Mendacity." Personally, I don't know what good we do ourselves letting them print that kind of talk; I mean it doesn't make our jobs any easier. And I don't know how Elroy was able to get into our work release center anyway; he served only eleven years for beating a man to death and all, a U.S. soldier to boot. But at night in the office he has been very polite, sipping his coffee and talking about the different effects snow has on people and smiling all along like we are colleagues unwinding at a tea party together or something. He is usually always clean shaven, but these past few days he has let a white stubble come out on his perpetually red face. That is what I should have noticed: his change in hygiene habits combined with his new-found friendliness towards us staff members. Changes like that should be taken note of. They can mean an inmate's getting ready to do something drastic like escape, or maybe even kill himself: Douglas Agnes McElroy's too mean to kill himself.

I leave the second floor and walk down the iron staircase above the mess hall, shining my beam over the landing to check again the night crew's cleaning job; it looks good, gleaming in the light. I climb the north stairs to the third floor. The center is working at full capacity now so we're putting three men to a room: two in a bunk, one in a single bed. Up here the air is dry and smells like hot metal. All fall, and now winter, the heater has been working over-time. One night a while ago one of us staff members turned it up too high, and that night the inmates opened their windows to let in the cold air, which got the automatic thermostat cranking the heat so hard the furnace almost blew. Now it heats the whole building too much, especially the third floor here, and any inmate caught with his window open gets put on immediate restriction. I walk down the hall that we keep dimly lit and go into the bath-room that we keep brightly lit. There are three white sinks under three mirrors. Two of them look pretty scummy. I didn't check on the third-floor work crew tonight; Leon did. I walk around the corner to where the stalls are, but have to stop; the smell is horren-dous. The toilet roll spins then the paper tears. I knock on the door. "Who's in there?"

"Who the fuck's askin'?"

"Buck?"

"Norton?"

"Yeah, I'm doing a head check."

"Be right out."

I walk past the sinks around the opposite corner to where the showers are, pause to breathe some fresh air. The toilet flushes. Buck is the kind of inmate I can never quite get used to. I suppose it's because even though I know his crimes, I still can't keep from liking him. He's a biker, a leading officer in the southwestern chapter of Satan's Siblings. He's in on weapons violations and drug distribution charges and he weighs three hundred and thirty-two pounds. He has a gray-and-black beard that is longer than the ponytail that hangs down his back, and he has tattoos etched all over his huge body. He says he did most of the work himself while he was in prison, the parts he could reach anyway. He comes around the corner now, barefoot, hitching up his size forty-eight jeans, tucking in his super-large Harley-Davidson T-shirt. "What's the good word?"

"Not much. When'd you get in?"

"When you were upstairs groovin' on the gash." He bends over the sink and washes his hands and face, his stomach resting on the porcelain. "So old Elroy's jumped ship."

"Where'd you hear that?"

"Leon was on the phone with your big brother when I came in." He reaches for a paper towel and wipes his face and beard. "You already start escape procedure?"

"Buck."

"Al. Who the fuck am I gonna tell?"

"We started about an hour ago. The trooper just left."

"Trooper?"

"Come on, that's all I can say."

"Okay, kid." He crumples up the towel and drops it into the trash can, then lumbers past me into the hall down towards his room. I find his name on my clipboard and check it off. He's scummy as hell, but I do like him. I think it's because he's really on a straight road, at least while he's in here. He works a late shift down at a leather cutting shop in Denver, and he is one of the only inmates that Mark has given driving privileges. The rest take a bus for the twenty-mile ride to Denver, or else, if they're close enough, they walk to their jobs. That's where Elroy was supposed to be until ten-thirty tonight, at his second-shift job in a machine shop here in Boulder. Eleven o'clock is our late night curfew and that's not the one anybody should mess with. If an inmate works a night shift and has to work overtime, then he's supposed to call us right away to let us know. It's up to us to extend his curfew or not. If by eleven-thirty we haven't had contact with an inmate, then we start escape procedure. But really, we don't have too many of them; I've only handled one in the six months I've been here, and even that wasn't a genuine escape, but a death.

His name was Muddy River Johnson. Some of the others called him that because he used to get drunk all the time up in the canyons and fall into the Muddy River. He was a recovering alcoholic and a Vietnam combat veteran, which surprised me because he looked more like a World War II vet with his graying hair and the lines in his face and all. He was very gentle and soft-spoken for an inmate. Never had a bad word to say about anybody. One night on the way home from his dishwashing job at the Montview Hotel downtown, he had a heart attack and died. He was cutting through the park when he dropped. Nobody found him until seven the next morning. I called it in though. I thought he had escaped.

I leave the bathroom and start checking the men's rooms. Just about everybody's sleeping on top of their blankets tonight because of the heat up here. That makes it pretty easy to see who's who without shining a light in anyone's face and getting something thrown at you. I'm in the second to last room at the end of the hall. Raoul White has his radio turned up too loud. It's on a hard rock station and there's a song on now that's blasting out whining high-pitched notes from an electric guitar. I like this music too, but I swear, I don't know how these guys can sleep through this. I shine my light on his radio box on the floor next to his bunk, then find the volume knob and crank it down. Raoul turns over in his bunk. His eyes are glazed over with sleep, but he still manages to give me the cold stare.

"It's too loud, Raoul. Get earphones."

He turns back over on his side and I leave his room and check the rest.

I'm at the beginning of my career in corrections, but I've already noticed some definite patterns about these people. One: it is very rare to walk into an inmate's room and not see at least two or three full color magazine pictures of nude women taped to the walls, and most of them are wide open crotch shots. There's one room downstairs where you can't find the wall. Two: there is always, always a radio or TV going, even when there is nobody in the room to hear or see it. I told Leon my first couple of months here how I couldn't understand them needing all that noise all the time. He turned to me, stopped filling out a urine-sample form, and said, "It's 'cause they can't stand all the voices in their heads keep telling them what fuck-ups they are." Maybe. Three: inmates don't wash their feet. Or at least one out of every two doesn't. Honest to God, sometimes I'm tempted to let them open their windows, heating bill or not, just so I don't have to smell them. Four—and this surprised me the most when I started this work: a lot of inmates read the Bible. The New Testament. The Old Testament. The Saint Joseph's edition. All kinds. And what a strange feeling I get when I go through an incoming inmate's possessions and find a couple of Bibles in a cardboard box right next to a stack of *Hustler* and *Penthouse* and *High Times*.

I'm in Paxton's room now. He shares it with one other guy usually, but tonight, because we are full these days, there are three in here. I'm standing in the middle of the room and have my flashlight pointed at the mountain of meat that is Big Bill Paxton. He weighs two hundred and ninety-five pounds and is black. He is the largest guy in the house next to Buck, and I am staring at him because I can't believe that even a body the size of his can be making the incredible sounds I am hearing snortle out of his sleeping face. I'm beginning to feel bad about turning down Raoul's radio; this is worse. I look over at Glenn Peters and Russ Haywood sleeping in the bunk. Glenn's on top. He's got his body to the wall with his pillow pulled over his head. Russ is sleeping on his back in the bottom bunk. He's got a fresh tattoo on his chest. I can't see the detail of it now, but he showed it to me yesterday. Buck did it for him. I don't know what he charged and I'm surprised Russ's counselor let him do it. Buck did it right in the middle of his chest. It's a big green snake with a dragon's head breathing out red and purple fire. Over it, just under Russ's throat, it says, FUCK OFF, in blue letters. Under it is written: AND DIE. When Russ showed it to me yesterday he looked like he had just been told he could go home or something. He said: "Hey, Al, this is it, right? I mean, ain't this fucking *it?*" Russ is ten years older than I am, and he looks it too, with his black moustache and goatee, his hairy forearms; but he's not playing with a full deck at all. I look down at the dark patch of ink on his sleeping chest, shake my head, then mark off names and leave the room.

At the second-floor landing I check the gauge of the fire extinguisher. The needle is still on the high-pressure numbers. I walk down the stairs to the first floor past the closed doors of coun-selors' offices I've already checked, but stop and check them again. Wilson's nasal-blocked voice is coming from the office. He's just come in out of the cold for his one A.M. to nine A.M. shift. I check Tony Giordano's door, think of Elroy being Tony's client. I know he's going to be surprised. I walk into the office.

"There he is," Leon says, looking over at me from where he sits at the desk. It's December in Colorado but black Leon Mavery is wearing a purple short-sleeved shirt that shows all his lumps. "Everything cool, Mr. Norton?"

"No problems. Hi, Wil."

"Al."

I look at him still in his Alaskan fur-lined parka. His wire-rimmed glasses are all steamed up and he's got ice in his beard. Then I see the wet leather chaps strapped over his jeans. "You're riding your bike in this stuff?"

"Had to."

"You're nuts."

"That's Wilson," Leon says.

"You been briefed on Elroy's escape, Wil?"

"Yep."

"What do you think?" I ask.

"Me? I'm glad he did it. I hope he fucking freezes to death out there."

"Good chance," Leon says.

I hand my clipboard to Leon. "What did my brother have to say?"

"His exact words? He said, 'Fuck that ornery old son of a bitch.' He's calling his PO in the morning. You off?"

"Yep." I pull my leather jacket off the hook on the supply

closet door. Wilson sits down across from Leon and picks up the logbook to sign in. He looks up at me while I'm zipping up. "Who inventoried Elroy's gear?"

I look at Leon. Leon looks at Wilson then looks at me. I take off my jacket and hang it back on the hook before he can say anything. I'm the junior employee around here, and the youngest too, twenty-four. I get this kind of bull tossed at me all the time. But it's not just because of my age; it's because my brother runs this place.

ELROY LIVES—well, used to live—up here on the third floor. The ceiling is painted an aqua blue and slants down almost to the floor on two sides. There's a small square window set in the wall between them, and if I get down on my knees, I can look through it and see the occasional light of a cabin in the foothills just outside of town. I put my inventory sheet and box of trash bags on the dresser then stoop beneath the ceiling and sit on Elroy's impeccably made bed. Everywhere I look in this room things are in total order. His desk has nothing on it but a small lamp with a little blue light bulb in it, a jar of pens and pencils, and the yellow legal pad he composes all of his bullshit propaganda on. But they're on the desk in perfect arrangement, spaced equally apart, and the legal pad is set directly in front of the chair where at night I have seen him sitting, hunched over his desk, writing away under his blue light. Course, I've had to interrupt him at these times and tell him that it's lights out and to please hit the sack. The looks he has given me from his desk under his slanted ceiling in his blue light could kill, really. With his bushy eyebrows and gray hair and heavy shoulders, I have thought more than once that he resembles a troll under a bridge somewhere, a killer troll. But he has never said anything to me; he has just put his pen down on his pad, and with that look still on his face, turned off the light.

I looked away from the desk to the small bookshelf beside it. He built it himself. Not a bad job, I guess. I watched him whip it together this past September in the courtyard between the mess hall and the women's wing. He got a hammer and some nails and a handsaw and built it in about thirty minutes. But even then his face didn't change from that constant tight-jawed look it always has. I look over the titles of some of his books as I take them off the shelves: *Living My Life* by Emma Goldman; *Masonry for the Carpenter; The Paris Review; Farming Without Banks; The Unrevised Shakespeare;* 1984 by George Orwell. I skim through the last one. I read it in my freshman English course back at Syracuse five years ago. I see the words "The Ministry of Truth." I think about Elroy's essays to the house paper, about him putting down our president all the time, about him putting down us and the Department of Corrections. Screw you, Elroy.

I drop the books into a green trash bag then clear the shelves of the rest. On the bottom shelf is a pile of magazines, neatly stacked. There are some *National Geographic*s, a few copies of something called *Mother Jones,* and some of *Time* and *U.S. News & World Report.* But beneath them all, at the very bottom of the stack, is a worn and slightly tattered magazine called *African Mamas Sucking Hog.* I flip through it real quick; a bunch of young black girls dressed up like Kenyans giving fat-ass bikers blow jobs. I smile at this; Elroy the scholar. Elroy the sicko killer masturbator. I drop the magazine in the bag and tie it off then get another one and empty his drawers of all his clothes. There's not much; navy blue Dickey work pants and sweatshirts, white boxer shorts and socks, all matched and folded and set in the drawer alongside each other as neat as can be.

I move to his bedside table, pick up his white wind-up alarm clock, and drop it into the bag. Then I see something I have never noticed before: a small gold picture case, the kind that can fold up and fit in your pocket. I sit on the bed and look at the black-and-white picture in the oval frame. It's a family portrait taken outside somewhere. Elroy's standing in the middle with one arm around a woman, the other resting on the shoulder of a boy who looks to be around fifteen or sixteen. They are all dressed up. The woman is in a light-colored dress with some kind of flower pinned above her breasts, and McElroy and the boy are wearing dark jackets and pants with black ties and white shirts. Elroy's hair is completely black, not a gray hair anywhere, and he is squinting into the sunshine with an actual, honest-to-God smile on his face. The kid's got a crew cut and the same Cro-Magnon forehead as McElroy, but his hair is blond like the woman's. I close the case and put it into the bag on top of his clothes.

After I gather his shaving kit and legal pad and jar of pens and pencils, I tie off the second bag and start lugging them downstairs to the basement. When I get there I drop them and fumble with my security keys. The furnace rattles in the room next to me. I find the storage room key, unlock the door, flick on the light switch, and step into the tomb. That's what it feels like, a semisacred underground place for escaped, dead, or terminated inmates' belongings. The room is rectangular and the two long walls have storage bins built against them. But they're not really bins; they're made of wood and look more like the concrete coffin shelves you see in mausoleums. There are about twenty of these against both walls. I pick up McElroy's bags and drop them in front of an empty space beneath the shelf that holds Muddy River Johnson's trunk. I packed that myself. There's nothing in it but an old corduroy coat, a toothbrush, and a pair of army boots. Nobody has bothered to come by to pick it up. It'll probably be auctioned with the rest of the unclaimed belongings in May. Leon says I'd be a fool not to show up and bid against the guys from the sheriff's department for some of this stuff. I heave McElroy's bags into the shelf and write in his full name: Douglas Agnes McElroy, then the date: Tuesday, December 14, 1982.

In the office, Wilson is leaning back in his chair with his feet up on the desk reading a copy of *Time* magazine. Something smells awful, like a cross between piss and burning hair. I look around and see his chaps draped over the heating vent.

"Tough shift, Wilson."

"Screw."

"Where's Leon?"

"Gone."

"That makes two of us." I take my jacket off the hook, and when I pull it on and zip it up, Wilson lowers his magazine and says: "See you tomorrow, Al."

"Uh-uh. This is my weekend. See you Friday."

"Whatever." He raises his magazine back over his face and I leave the office, walk down the back hall, and pull my security keys off the brass ring clipped to my belt. On the first-floor landing I glance down at the mess hall and see the half-empty coffee cup on one of the tables, an opened Sweet 'N Low next to it. I go down the stairs, pick up the cup, crumple up the sweetener pack, and wipe the table off with my hand. I really don't care if these animals have a clean dining room or not, but I don't want Wilson thinking I can't handle night clean up detail. I put the cup in the rack that's set in the wall then turn to check for any other messes. There's a Christmas tree in the corner, a big one, some kind of native Colorado spruce. Raoul White and another inmate work a day job with a logger near Loveland. They cut it down and brought it in for everybody. Mark let Tony and Sherry Anne buy some new Christmas lights for it, and they had Maggie and Paulina put them on the tree. But there are no other decorations on it, just the lights, and right now they're not even plugged in.

I unlock the door and step into the night, pushing back on the door handle until it clicks then pulling it to make sure. I put on my wool cap and walk down the concrete path that is dry except for strips of ice here and there. Up the side street at the corner in front of the house, the cruiser is gone. Crusty piles of snow line both sides of Tenth Avenue; they glitter under the streetlight, and I yawn and think of my electric blanket and bed. In the back alley Wilson's motorcycle leans against the building in front of my Monte Carlo. He's got it chained to the iron railing of the back stairs; there's ice on the chain; Wilson's soft in the head. I unlock my door then get in fast and start her up. I put on my seat belt, rev the engine a couple of times, turn on the headlights, then flick on my wipers so I can see. They flap in front of me but the fog on the windshield stays. I start to wipe it off with the back of my hand but then stop. I sit still. My whole car smells like booze. I take a breath then turn right around into a hand that grabs my face and squeezes my cheeks so tight my molars are about to cave into my mouth. I see a big knife blade about three inches from my face. Then I am looking into eyes I know. They are glassy. Wide-set beneath bushy gray eyebrows. They are mean; they belong to Elroy.

"Hello, Alley Oop. How are you?"

I don't say anything. I don't try. He holds the knife up for me to see.

"This is a very sharp knife, Al. Do you know what kind it is?"

My teeth are stinging my cheeks. I shake my head as best I can.

"I thought not. It's a Bowie knife, Al. I have castrated horses with knives like this. They do the trick. Believe me."

His breath hits me straight in the nose.

"Now I am going to let go of your face, Allen. And when I do, you are not goin' to move. You get me?"

I nod my head. My eyes are watering.

"Good."

He loosens his grip then lets go completely. I take a deep breath and rub my jaw with my hand. I see myself jerking open my door and running out into the alley and around to the front door and Wilson, but I can't move. He leans between the bucket seats and holds the knife loosely in his hand. It is huge.

"We're going on a little trip, kid. Put this car in gear. I'll direct you."

"Mr. McElroy—"

"Shut up. Just back this car up and drive down the alley to Broadway Street."

I put her in gear and back over the potholes behind me. When the car jolts a little I almost apologize. I've got to stay calm. I look once to my left, at the white brick wall of the center, at Wilson's motorcycle. Then I drive straight ahead between the back-door lots of fraternity houses. I look to see if a party is going on in the ground floor of any of them, but everywhere there are dark rooms and closed curtains. My mouth is all dust inside.

"Take a slow and careful left when you get to Broadway, Al."

Elroy's voice has never sounded so low and rough. I stop where the alley intersects Broadway and look to my right up the hill where there are streetlights and Pau-Pau's Variety Store. Across from that are the tall pine trees surrounding the university campus. The university police.

"Left."

I see the knife turn a little bit. I put on my indicator, wait for a green Jeep to pass me, then pull out onto the street and head down the hill towards the shopping district.

"How much petrol have you got, Al?"

"Half a tank."

"That'll be enough for now," he says as he squeezes his body between the seats and sits beside me with a grunt. "That's better, Al. Yes, it is." He lowers the knife and I feel it press against my side on the outside of my jacket. He reaches behind him between the seat and the door and pulls a bottle from the back. It's brown and shaped funny. He takes a sip then points straight ahead with a thick crooked finger.

"You just take another slow and careful right turn when you get to the corner before the bank. Take that right and then get on 119 to Niwot. And Al, do not fuck with me. I am in complete control of my senses."

2

My mind is one big training manual. I'm seeing white pages flip over and over in my head; I'm trying to remember anything I might have read about being kidnapped by an inmate under your jurisdiction, how to handle a knife. My palm slips slightly as I take the turn in front of Rocky Mountain Bank. There is a red traffic light in front of us. I have to stop. Okay, I'll speed the car up just a little then jam on the brakes and put Elroy through the windshield. I see it all clearly in my head but my body isn't going along with it. I pull the car to a gentle stop in front of the red light, look to my left, past the darkened parking lot of the bank, to the outdoor mall, where just yesterday I saw a movie before I came to work: *Star Wars*. McElroy takes another swig off of his bottle, the knife point pushing at my side. I don't believe this. The light changes and I drive straight ahead.

"We might have some fun tonight, Al. You never can tell."

"We should talk about this, McElroy."

"Talk?"

"Yes, *talk*. You are escaping from a correctional facility, Elroy. You are kidnapping a corrections em*ploy*ee. Jesus Christ, they'll lock you up forever."

"*Wrong.*" He pushes the blade a bit more into my jacket. "You've got that wrong, Allen."

"I know. I'm sorry. You're right."

He takes another drink and I keep my mouth shut.

We go through seven more traffic lights before we are out of the city and driving alone in the darkness up two-laned 119 towards Niwot. At the third traffic light, the one right before The Rhino, I almost did it. The blade had pulled far enough away from my side so that I didn't even feel it, but when I leaned forward a little to prepare myself I felt my seat belt pulling across my chest. I went limp as I tried to imagine getting free of the belt and opening the door before Elroy had time to put it in me. And I couldn't take the seat belt off before I hit the brakes or I'd go through the windshield with him. So that plan is out. But right now, I'm not thinking about plans. Elroy's keeping that foot-long, two-and-a-half-inch blade right at my side. I'm almost afraid that if I do think up something, the thought will travel down through my body, be picked up by that Bowie, absorbed into Elroy's hand then brain and *slice*—that'll be all she wrote. So I'm just sitting here with both hands on the wheel looking straight ahead at my headlights cutting through the darkness, lighting up this road that passes over the flatlands of Colorado just east of the foothills. On either side, as far as you can see, is white frozen snow about a foot deep and a week old. If it were daytime I could look out of my window to my left and see a blue-gray wall of mountains looming out of the fields on the horizon. I know this because just last Saturday when I was working I had to drive up here to monitor a furlough, Maggie Nickerson's.

"You're doing just fine, Allen. I want you to know that."

"Do you think you could pull the knife away then?"

"Yes, Al, I can do that, and will, but when we get into Niwot you can count on it being pretty close."

"What are we going to do there?"

"That's my concern, kid. Not yours."

His voice just went down a notch, but he keeps his knife in his lap. I can see a ball of light up ahead in the distance: Niwot. It looks to be three or so miles more. I sit tight and drive and keep my mouth shut, but I'm watching him as best I can out of the corner of my eye. He looks a lot smaller sitting in a car seat. With his sloping shoulders and his short torso, he almost looks like a monkey, but old, dangerous, too. He's wearing his thick winter-lined dungaree jacket, and he has on a blue workshirt with a T-shirt underneath. We're driving under the streetlights on the far outskirts of Niwot and I can see his face better. His chin is jutted out forward a little like when he takes out his teeth, and his eyes are narrowed so that there are real deep furrows in the skin of his forehead; he looks like he might be pondering some kind of deep philosophical question, but I know he's just trying to keep his booze in line. I look down at the brown bottle in his lap: Grand Marnier. It sounds like something a sailor would drink. Drink up then, Elroy. Guzzle yourself to death.

"You know that I used to teach literature, don't you, Al?"

He snaps that question at me so fast I jerk a little bit in my seat.

"What's the matter, boy?"

"Nothing, I just—"

"You just don't expect me to be cognitively in charge, isn't that it, Al?"

"Whatever you say." I look at him for a second and he is looking back at me, smiling.

"Yes. I taught literature at Greeley. Now I'm no writer, but I do know literature. The Elizabethan period is my specialty, Al. And Al. Do not think for a second that one little bottle of French liqueur is goin' to rob me of my senses and render me stupid."

"We're in Niwot."

"That is correct." He puts that huge knife point to my jacket side. "There's a Sunoco station up here to your right. It's full service." He lowers the liquor bottle down between his legs onto the floor, and I pull in alongside the pumps. Dirty snow is plowed up against the side of the building. A young guy is inside reading a magazine. He's leaning back in a chair and has his feet up on his desk. I honk the horn and the kid looks up then stands to get his coat that's hanging behind him. I think about Wilson, about how maybe he should have noticed my fogged-up windows in the back alley when he pulled up on his motorcycle. Maybe he could have looked and thought about it for just one second. Elroy slips the knife between the car seat and where my kidneys are as the kid comes out of the building. He's rubbing his hands together and his breath is shooting out in front of him in short foggy blasts.

"Mornin'," he says.

I'm about to speak but then Elroy leans in front of me. "Fill it up, son."

"Yessir."

A frigid breeze is coming in steady through the window. I start to reach for the handle. "Mind if I roll the window up?"

"Yes, I do, Al. That air is good for you. Keep you awake. Get out your money."

I reach around and get my wallet. He takes it from me then opens it and takes out all I got, a twenty and two ones.

"I didn't think you were making millions over at Fascist House."

I sit there in the cold, smelling gasoline. The attendant hangs up the nozzle, then comes around to the window.

"Eight-seventy."

Elroy presses that Bowie flat against my lower back as he leans in front of me and hands the kid my twenty. "Hey partner, I wonder if you'd be willing to bring us four black coffees from your machine I see in there. I'd be happy to give you a couple extra dollars for your trouble."

I'm looking straight into this kid's face. He's got a few pink pimples on his chin and forehead, and I'm looking right into his watery brown eyes, moving mine all around then shooting them in the direction of Elroy beside me. The kid just smiles at me like he understands how it is to be with senile grandfathers or something. Then he says, "Sure. No problem."

IT WAS JUST AFTER Elroy had me get off 119 past Longmont, heading north on Highway 25, when I realized nobody would be missing me for at least two whole days. I'm not due back at the center until Friday, so unless someone saw a gray-haired man pop my car door lock then climb into my Monte Carlo with a huge knife in his hand, nobody would connect us. When this hit me, my heart started beating fast and my hands got slick on the wheel. I leaned forward a little in my seat to take a breath but then spilled coffee between my legs onto my crotch. A hot wave passed through me and for a second I felt like I was going to throw up. All of this Elroy didn't seem to notice; he just kept sitting there in the dark holding his Styrofoam cup of coffee in one hand, his Bowie knife in the other, leaning his head back against the seat and watching the white lines of route 25 come into my headlight space then pass under us like they were medicine for his old bones, water for a man in the desert. But then he turned to me and said: "No one will be looking for a sky blue Monte Carlo for two days anyway, will they, Al?" And I couldn't say anything. Not a word came from my lips. And in the back of my head somewhere I realized I had been hoping that this hadn't been planned at all, that he had just jumped off the wagon after work and flipped out, that after he sobered up he was bound to calm down, realize how rash he had been, and have me drive him back to face the music. But then what about the knife? I hadn't been letting myself think about that. Now that is all I am thinking about. If he's smart enough to rip off a car and a driver nobody's going to miss for forty-eight hours, if that's part one, then what's part two? And as we pass through the tiny sleeping town of Rimnath heading towards Bellington, my throat dry from coffee, my palms slippery with sweat, I just turn to him and ask him straight out, "Are you going to kill me, Elroy?"

He looks at me and I can barely make out his expression in the early morning darkness, but I know that it has changed. That look isn't on his face anymore, and his eyes have softened somehow, like all of a sudden nothing is funny to them or ever will be again.

"I do not enjoy killing, Al. It is not a hobby for me."

I look back at the road and hear him sip from his bottle.

"Though I have done it, haven't I? As a soldier and a civilian I have done it. Just make sure you do it wearing their colors is all I can say. 'Cause mister, if you don't—"

I look at him for a second. He is looking straight at me. I look back at the road.

"You are a cage keeper, Al. I can see you take your job seriously, too. You want to be a good cage keeper. Maybe someday run one like your brother, Mark, back at Fascist House. You are a good cop, Al. That is what you want to be. Just don't try being one now, kid. I do not fancy the idea of snuffing you out, but I will if you start to play hero with me. I will slit you open like a fish."

I look at him then look back at the road, then look at him again. "You won't get any trouble from me, Mr. McElroy."

He nods without a word and I go back to my driving. I want to check my watch but he still has his eyes on me; I don't want him to wonder anything crazy. The sky is still very dark, no beginning signs of daybreak, but it can't be more than a couple hours away. We pass through Bellington, just a short stretch of one-room stores with faded lettering in their windows, some framed with Christmas lights that cast orange and red and blue onto the empty sidewalk. We come to an intersection with a blinking yellow light and I keep going but up ahead on the left is a brightly lit Winchell's Donuts. The only customer in it is a very fat police officer sitting at the counter with his back to the glass.

"Don't even think of speeding up or doing anything else to attract that pig's attention."

That huge horse castrater is at my side. I look away from the doughnut shop as we leave Bellington and enter again the darkness of route 25 heading north.

I HAVE NEVER BEEN IN Wyoming before, I am there now. We passed through Cheyenne shortly before five o'clock this morning and were out of there in no time. The highway runs to the west of it and as we passed this flat frontier metropolis, I looked past Elroy's caveman profile to the still-lighted streetlamps at the base of the buildings; I saw the red taillights of a Trailways bus that was heading down one of the streets towards the center of the city and I thought then how I would like to be on that bus, how I have always liked buses, how I slept on one almost the whole day-and-a-half trip down to Fort Lauderdale with Gus and Lopes spring break our sophomore year. While I slept they drank beer that we had smuggled in after a stop in Georgia. But I just couldn't stay awake in the soft jolts and vibrations of that moving bus. That's what I thought of as this cutthroat bastard and I passed Cheyenne and hit the snow prairies of Wyoming just in time for sunrise. At first there was a pale lip of pink on the horizon. Then the sun was totally exposed, looking as orange and round as an egg yolk. Now it is daylight and I find myself driving alongside men and women in cars and trucks and vans on their way to work. I look over at McElroy and he is looking at me. I wonder how long he has been doing that. Then I see him stick his thumb and forefinger into his mouth and pull out his teeth. He wipes them on his pant leg but keeps his bloodshot eyes on me. The center of his face just caved into the gaping hole under his nose. He looks like a lamprey eel. I look back at the road as he clicks his teeth into his mouth, then sits up and spits something onto the floor of my car.

"There is a plan here, Al. There *is* a plan." He looks at me, waiting for my reaction like we're two chums on a vacation together or something. "We're going straight up into Canada, kid. You are goin' to drive. But we will travel only by night. We will sleep by day. The border can't be more than seven hundred miles north of us if I am not mistaken, course we will have to get a map. Do you have a map?"

I shake my head, though I think my Rand-McNally is still folded up in my glove compartment.

"No matter." He puts the knife between his legs and rubs his hands together. He looks out the windshield then reaches over and turns off the heat. "With luck and proper precautions I see no reason why you can't have me safely in the province of Saskatchewan by midmorning tomorrow." He picks up the knife again and then points it straight ahead at the highway. "I want you to pull into the next rest area. That is all you need to know for now." He lowers the Bowie to his lap and I look to my right hoping somebody might have seen this ugly man with the bushy gray eyebrows waving a knife around. I see a guy in an orange Datsun 240 Z. He is looking straight at us but not with the expression of someone concerned. He's got on glasses and is going bald. His shirt collar is too tight for his neck. He looks like my dad.

We are halfway to Casper before I see a rest area sign and get into the right lane to exit. I glance at my watch. It's seven twenty-two. We are driving through some of the flattest country I have ever seen, and it's all covered with snow. A sign says: WHEATLAND 8 MILES. I pull into the rest area, a plowed parking lot lined with a few trees. There's a concrete rest-room building in the middle and Elroy has me go way off in the corner away from a parked eighteen wheeler. I pull in under the snow-weighted branch of a tall spruce and I think of the Christmas tree standing in the corner of the mess hall back at the center. I'm tired. My bladder's full. I don't even feel very scared right now.

"We will both go to the latrine, Al. You will walk in front of me. That trucker is fast asleep in his rig, so you can stop thinking of him coming to your rescue. Also, I am quite adept at throwing this knife and making it stick. Get the picture?"

"Yes."

"Good. Get out of the car after me."

After we finish urinating and splashing water on our faces Elroy has me open my trunk to see I don't know what. He lifts my spare tire and looks at the empty space beneath it. Then he opens my toolbox and rummages through that. There's a slow wind coming from the ice fields behind the rest room. It's going right through my jacket. It's freezing the water left over on my face. I look at Elroy bending over into my trunk then think of myself taking one step forward and slamming the lid down on his head. My blood's rushing through my temples as I see it happening, but again, my body doesn't make a move. Then he finds what I forgot I had there: a short coil of heavy tow rope Mark lent me this past August after my car stalled for the second time in downtown Denver. Elroy straightens then closes the trunk, his knife handle sticking out of his heavy jeans jacket pocket, my brother's rope in his hand.

"Get in the front seat, Al. It's bedtime."

IN THE LAST SIX or seven hours I have probably slept two. My leather jacket is bunched up between my shoulder blades. My toes are frozen solid. And I see my breath shoot in front of me every time I exhale. Right now I'm looking straight up past my steering wheel and out of my windshield at the branches of the spruce tree we parked under. I can see the sky through them. It must be around two or three o'clock, though the way my hands are tied to the steering wheel I don't feel like straining my neck muscles to check my watch and see. The rope runs down my body, joins my feet and legs together, and is tied to the armrest of the passenger door. My legs are bent up in a right angle and my butt is resting on the hump between the seats. Elroy's got the remaining rope tied to his wrist in the back, or so he told me just before he went to sleep. He is the most quiet sleeper I have ever not heard. You can hardly hear him breathe even. More than once I shined my light in his sleeping face back at the center just to make sure he hadn't died. And more than once he would wake up cussing about his civil rights and invasion of privacy and every other piece of legal horse-shit that came to his immediately alert brain. But no such luck now; he is definitely alive and breathing in the backseat of my car. I can feel it through the rope.

A little while after he nodded off I heard the eighteen wheeler start up. I prayed that the driver would pull close enough to my car to look down and catch a glimpse of a guy tied up in the front seat. But he just meshed his gears and was gone. Now, hours later, the insides of all the windows are fogged up with my and Elroy's breathing. So nobody's going to see us by accident unless they open a door, which is what I am hoping now, that a passing state trooper will pull in to check on the lone parked car with the misted-over windows. But I can't even concentrate on that. My mind is just bouncing around from one wired thought to another. I still can't forgive myself for not clocking Elroy with the trunk lid. One hard whack; that's all it would've taken. Or I could have at least pulled the knife out of his jacket pocket and thrown it onto the highway, then made a run for it. I hear the cars passing by and I think of all those Jews who just climbed into those trains knowing they were being sent to their deaths. I remember seeing film footage of that in a sociology course back at Syracuse. There must have been one hundred people to each Nazi with a machine gun, but nobody even gave the guy eye contact. They just helped each other into the cattle cars without a word. I couldn't understand that then. I've always kind of agreed with the old adage that right makes might. I'm not sure about all of that tied up in the cold of my own car though. I know I'm right but I can't seem to make a move around this animal who, with his bare hands, beat to death some innocent guy on an army base a few years ago. And I don't even know if it's just fear that keeps paralyzing me. But I do know this: I've got to let myself sleep. I've got to rest and clear my head. The cold's not bothering me much anymore. Except for my fingers and nose, I feel sufficiently numb all over. I close my eyes and breathe deeply. The caffeine has worn off and my heart has slowed back down to normal. With each breath I'm telling every frozen muscle in my body to let go. At least my wool cap is still on my head. I think of my eighth-grade teacher, Ms. Farnes, telling us how forty percent of a person's body heat can leave an uncovered head. I see and hear other people in my life. The voices of some are in the mouths of others. Then I am no longer tied up in the front seat of my Monte Carlo; I see my father getting out of our station wagon. I have been playing one-on-one with Mark and am all sweaty and dirty and feel good. My father's tie is loosened and his collar is unbuttoned. His glasses are in his left shirt pocket, but not in his case. He looks sick, like he is about to throw up, and I can see that his eyes are red. I say: "Hey Dad, what're you, sloshed?" He turns towards me, then walks as steadily as any human being ever walked in his life. He hugs me harder than he ever hugged me before. He looks over my head at Mark coming out of the house, the screen door slamming behind him, then, in words that don't have enough air behind them, he says, "Oh sweet Jesus. Somebody has killed your mother."

HUNGER IS WHAT woke me. Hunger and cold. My eyes feel like two desert pools dried up in my head, so I know I haven't slept enough. The car smells like Elroy's booze breath and I can't see through the frost of the windshield, but night has definitely fallen. I stretch my neck and turn my wrist through the rope. It's six-seventeen on my digital watch. I let my head fall back and my cap comes off. I can't remember ever being this hungry before. I think the circulation has been cut off in my hands and feet. And my butt has frozen itself to the hump between the seats. I want to clear my bowels and brush my teeth. I can't hear Elroy's breathing but, again, that's nothing new. I rest my head back on my cap and think of sticking that huge Bowie into his gut when I hear somebody whistling outside. It's a cheerful dopey tune; something Roy Rogers would whistle to Trigger. Christ, maybe it's a cop. The back door opens, the ceiling light goes on, and Douglas Agnes McElroy sticks his head inside.

"Rise and shine, Alley Oop. You got some driving to do." He leans in between the bucket seats, puts the Bowie handle between his teeth, then unties my feet. He gets the knot loosened on my hands and as soon as he pulls the rope away from my wrists, he takes the knife from his mouth and rests the point of it on my chin. "I'm figuring it feels like the real thing to you now, son. Do not forget what I told you about playing hero with me. I propose to get through this all right. I suggest you do the same."

"I'm hungry."

"We will go take care of our toiletries. Food will be our first priority after that."

THERE IS SOMETHING about ordering food from a plastic clown when you've got a convicted murderer at your side with his Bowie pressed against your jacket that makes you feel you might have died and gone to another planet. I got over this feeling and ordered four super-large tacos and two large Cokes from what sounded like a high school girl. When I pulled around to the pickup window she looked down and smiled at me and told me the price again: six fifty-seven. Her eyes were dark brown and so was her hair, but she had thin pale arms that seemed out of place when you saw how large her breasts were. She reminded me of Angela Nickerson, Maggie's daughter, and when I handed her my money I didn't even give her a signal that things weren't so cool in my car. I just looked into her eyes, dark as a deer's, and thought about that little homemade Christmas tree in Maggie's room back at the center. I thought of that, and Angela, and pieces of her father's skull lying on the floor at her feet, and how I hadn't shaved or brushed my teeth and would like to. And when she gave me my change, handed me my food, and smiled her business smile, I couldn't smile back. I was looking at her thin arms holding that bag of food out in the winter air for me to take, and I thought how weak they looked, how they seemed to be straining with just the weight of a few tacos and a couple Cokes. I was staring at a little brown mole on her white forearm and went into a gaze, one of those times when your mind and eyes just decide to lock in on something then space out on you until you can almost feel the drool on your chin. "Here's your food, sir."

McElroy nudged me with the knife and I took the bag, put the car in gear, and got back on the highway. But I was still in some other focus. Elroy handed me a taco but as starved as I was I didn't eat it right away. I sipped my Coke through a straw, looked straight ahead at the taillights of cars full of people who had homes to go to, and thought of my mother. I saw her getting into the little red Opel Sport my dad had given her as a present for their sixteenth wedding anniversary. I saw her getting into that in front of our house, driving up the street, stopping, waiting for a car to pass, then taking a right. This I saw walking up from where the high school bus had just dropped me off. It's the last action I ever saw my mother make. It's what I see instead of memories— warm greeting card memories you are supposed to have of dead people you love. Laughter and tears. Home-cooked meals. All that shit. I don't see any of that. I just see my mother drive a hundred yards, stop, then take a right to her destiny, to some punk who snatches her purse then shoves her through a plate-glass window before he runs and gets away, that's right, never gets caught. And my mother's sweet head is just about severed on the floor of Adler's pharmacy in downtown Syracuse.

My brother Mark was a junior at Syracuse University then. For about a month he and Frank Walters and another friend of theirs, John McLaughlin, they drove the streets looking, just looking. Twice they beat the shit out of kids because they wore leather jackets and carried big radios that they had probably stolen anyway. But then Mark almost got busted for drunk driving, stopped cruising for revenge, and became a hermit student. He changed his major from business to criminal justice. He said he wanted to be a cop but then he met Anne and married her a month before they both graduated. She told him she would not be one of those women who wait up nights to find out whether her husband has been shot down in the streets or not. So now Mark runs the tightest community corrections center in the mountain region. All of the inmates hate him there. They call him King Screw. But he's got respect. He tells me community corrections is just a stepping-stone for him to penitentiary work. He wants to be a kick-ass warden. Then, who knows? Maybe even run for office. Get capital punishment legislation passed in every state in the country.

That's how he's handling things. And I guess I've taken a similar road. I have always wanted to be like Mark, not in every way, but in most. For me a criminal justice career became inevitable, was kind of an organic reaction to the new family I found myself living in all through the rest of high school and into college. My father, who never fired a weapon after his time in the army back in the early fifties, he's got a complete arsenal now: shotguns, rifles, and ten kinds of handguns. Soon after my mother's funeral he joined a rod and gun club, and after he became proficient with his first purchase, a .357-magnum revolver, he started taking us down to the range to learn too. Every Wednesday and Saturday afternoon for almost a year my father, Mark, and I would go down to the club, put earphones over our heads, then for close to an hour we would blow away the shadowed silhouettes of men hanging from the north wall of the place. My father started drinking less, even socially, and stepped up his tennis playing from just once or twice a week to five or six times. That's where he met Julie, down at the Maple Leaf Health Club. She's ten years older than I am and six years older than Mark. She's been with my dad for five years now. Whenever they go out on the town for the night my dad carries his .380 semiautomatic in his pants pocket. It's small enough and flat enough it's not conspicuous, and he can get it out of his pocket pretty fast. One night he drew it on a kid who stepped around the corner of Luigi's restaurant to ask for a light.

I reach between the bucket seats for my second taco and napkin when my headlights light up a green sign that says: CASPER 49 MILES. Elroy hasn't said a word since before the Jack in the Box, but he just burped without covering his mouth; it's the Elroy I know and hate. The anarchist essayist. The silent killer troll. Fuck you, Elroy. Just see how much farther I drive you, you sonuvabitch. I wipe my face, look straight ahead, and sip from my Coke. Then Elroy opens the glove compartment and pulls out my Rand-McNally map. He stares at it, kind of weighs it in his hand, then looks straight ahead and says: "Pull the car over, Al." His voice is low and steady. I get into the breakdown lane and stop. I wait a second then turn to face him when his fist slams into my left eye, snapping my head back against the window. Then he is holding me by my jacket collar, touching his knife to my throat.

"I have lived without insurance all my life, kiddie cop. I can finish it now. I can cut your fucking throat right this second. It is up to you."

"I forgot it was there. I swear." I am looking into his steely eyes. They look hurt. I feel nothing.

He lets go of my jacket. "Get out at the same time I do."

We get out of my car together. Cars light us up as they pass us. A freezing wind hits me in the face. My eye aches. It's closing up.

"Come over here."

I walk around the front of the car to the passenger door and Elroy. The wind is blowing his gray hair back from his face, and his eyes are red and watery. I get inside, and as he ties my hands and feet and leaves the rest of the coil in front of me, I think how crazed he looks. He still smells like that French booze, but it's gotten worse after sitting inside his guts. He smells like sweet formaldehyde and sweat.

We're back on the highway and Elroy's driving, hunched up behind the wheel. "I guess I'm just about the lowliest creature you've ever come across, Al."

"One of them."

"You're being generous, kid. It's not like you."

"I didn't say you were a frigging saint, did I?"

"Oh well, then what am I?"

I'm looking straight ahead out of my right eye. My left is completely puffed out and closed up. "A murderer."

"That's not what they called me in Normandy, kid."

"You never got any medals. I read your file. You're a failed farmer and a half-assed carpenter who drinks too much and kills people."

He whacks my chest with the back of his fist. "Watch your fucking mouth, pig boy. I am old enough to be your goddamned gran'daddy."

"My grandfather would never kill an American soldier just for the hell of it."

"That's it." He extends his arm and presses the blade against my throat. "I do not want to hear another word come out of your young totalitarian sheep of a mouth. You get me?"

"Yes."

He pulls the knife away and I let out my breath, look straight ahead at the traffic we've gotten into. We're getting closer to Casper. Elroy reaches down and turns on the radio. He plays with the knob until he hears an organ squeezing out "White Christmas" and I lay my head against the seat and close my right eye to give it a rest from doing all the work. I forgot about the holidays; maybe because I'm scheduled to work Christmas Eve and Christmas Day, I don't know. Most everybody at the center got furloughs to friends' and relatives' anyway. The list of those who didn't was a lot shorter than those who did. Elroy was one of those who didn't. Typed next to his name was: No Available Sponsor. No shit.

I feel the car slowing down. I open my eye and see we're taking an exit. There's an Exxon station at the end of the ramp, a 7-Eleven next to it. Elroy gets off the ramp than pulls right into the gas station. I don't believe this: my eye is closed up, my hands and feet are tied, and he's pulling into an oasis of light.

"Give me your credit card, Al."

"I don't have one."

He parks the car under the self-service sign then pushes my head down to my knees. He pulls my wallet out of my back pocket and empties it. I sit up straight as he picks up my corrections ID. "DOB, 1958." He looks at me and squints his eyes at my beat-up face, then he looks down at my ID again and shakes his head. He goes through the rest of my wallet and only pauses to look over my firearms identification card. Then he finds the Brandt Studio picture of me and Dad and Mom and Mark. He holds it up in the light.

"Pretty lady."

"She's dead."

He cocks his head at me, his slits-for-eyes weighing the possible truth of what I just said. He puts the picture back in my wallet, drops it on my tied-up hands, and starts tapping the steering wheel with his knife. He looks out the windshield at the lights of the 7-Eleven on the other side of a snowbank and shakes his head. "Allen Norton. Why, oh why, don't you have any credit cards? How in *hell* are we going to get to Saskatchewan like this?"

I don't say a word.

"You've heard of the seven *p*'s, haven't you, kid? Well, I could have planned this escape just a wee bit better, but I thought for damn sure you'd be a credit card carrier. Well, that's that. We're going to have to resort to the Desperate Clause."

"Excuse me?"

"That's right, Al. We are goin' to have to commandeer some cash."

"Count me out."

He lifts his knife and studies the way the fluorescent light from above the gas pumps hits it. He takes a deep breath and lets out a lot of air. "Allen, do you really think I killed a man 'just for the hell of it'?"

He's holding his Bowie the way schoolyard bullies hold loose-clenched fists just before they sucker you. I don't answer.

"Do you?"

"I didn't read all of your file, Elroy."

"Is that what you do to understand a man; you consult the written records of the powers that be?"

"I guess not."

"You guess not." He turns to face me. "You're going to get us some cash."

"No, I'm not."

"Yes, you will." He reaches over and turns my tied wrists until he can see my glowing watch. "Eight thirty-four. We've got a three-and-a-half-hour wait." He digs into my pants pocket, pulls out the rest of my money, and counts it. "Two dollars and seventy-seven cents." He gets his wallet from his back pocket and takes out four ones. "We've got enough for a twelve-pack anyway." He tugs my cap down over my swollen and throbbing left eye, then drives away from the pumps into the 7-Eleven lot and parks right next to the snowbank away from the light of the store where he turns off everything then sticks all of that Bowie into a hole in the inside lining of his jeans jacket. He looks at me, takes my cap, then puts it on his head and rolls it up tight around the edges like sailors do. Flipping up his jacket collar, looking at himself in the rearview mirror, he rubs the white stubble on his chin. "Handsome motherfucker, don't you think?"

I watch him with my good eye as he enters the store and walks down one of the aisles to the glass beer coolers in the rear. There's a heavy middle-aged-looking woman with black frizzy hair sitting behind the counter. She turns her head to Elroy a second then goes back to watching the tiny black-and-white TV on top of the cash register. Elroy takes a twelve-pack out of the cooler then turns and walks to the other side of the store where I can't see him. I imagine he's checking out the camera situation or something. My eye really aches now. God*damn,* where are the police when you need them? Go on Elroy, do something in there that'll make that woman call the cops, anything, you half-assed murdering prick. I see him again. He walks to the counter, places the beer on it, and pulls the last of my money, and his, out of his front jeans pocket. The fat woman rings up the amount then takes the money and bags the beer without even looking at Elroy. She sits down and glues herself back to the TV as he picks up the bag and leaves the store.

Back in the car, Elroy pulls out two beers and drops one in my lap.

"I don't want it."

"Suit yourself." He pops open his, downs half of it, then wipes his mouth. "It's awful quiet in there, Al."

"So."

"Don't get mouthy with me, Norton." He keeps his eyes on me for a second then sips from his beer and looks through the windshield at the TV woman behind the counter of the store. "Now I fucked up, it's true. I didn't exactly plan this trip over a long period of time." He turns to look at me. "In fact, it just sort of came with the Grand Marnier."

"Then let's turn around and go back right now."

"You know nothing's ever that easy, kid. I'm surprised at you."

"Stop now, McElroy. Man, you don't even have any money. How are you going to make it in Canada without having to commit another felony there, too?"

"You don't understand, Allen. I am through playing life by lesser men's rules." He interrupts himself, finishes his beer, tosses the empty onto the backseat, then starts the car and backs out of the lot onto the street. "If we're goin' to rob this place, we sure as hell can't sit in the front of it drinking beer 'til we're ready."

We drive down the road away from the highway and store and gas station. We pass through a neighborhood full of split-level houses that are all lit up with Christmas lights. One's got a full-sized sleigh and a big plastic reindeer on its snow-covered roof. Inside the sleigh is a stuffed dummy in a Santa Claus suit. Red and green lights outline the whole thing. I see that through my good eye. Then the houses thin out until we're on a lone stretch of road in the dark. There's a utility station up ahead on the right, a short square cinderblock building with a tall chain-link fence all around it. My headlights light it up as Elroy pulls off the road and parks around the back alongside a fresh-plowed snowbank. He turns off the engine and lights.

"It's snowing, Al. Good sign."

"I hadn't noticed," I say as I see the tiny white crystals land then skitter over the windshield. "Why's that a good sign, McElroy?"

"Snow is a blanket, kid. A cover." He reaches in the backseat for another beer and I think of the Bowie knife in the lining of his jacket.

"Don't you like beer, Alley Oop?"

"Yes."

"Well drink one then. You're off duty."

"No, thank you."

"Help you get your nerve up."

"For what?"

"Don't play dumb with me."

"Look, I don't steal from people, all right?"

"God damn I can't believe you really exist, Allen. Nope. I take that back. I *know* you exist. You, and a whole generation like you. Boy, it's what we deserve, isn't it?"

"Who's we?"

"Americans."

"What do you have against Americans, Elroy? I mean, Jesus, if you don't like us why don't you go live someplace else? Like Russia for example."

He lowers his beer and looks at me in the dark. "I am goin' to let you talk to me like that only for the sake of enlightenment: yours. I know that you are looking at a man you have put into a comfortable little pigeonhole: convicted murderer, end of story. But that is not the end of the story, Allen. No, it is not." He drinks from his beer and I move my fingers back and forth to keep the circulation going. I think of how thick and crooked Elroy's are, like he has worked with them all his life. I remember the barn in that little oval portrait of his sitting in a garbage bag in the basement of the center, half a state away and so long ago, the words

No Available Sponsor typed next to Elroy's name on the Christmas furlough list. "Where's your family?" I ask.

"That chapter is no more, Al. That one is over."

He tosses the empty behind me then reaches into my lap and opens the one he dropped there. We are quiet for a while and my eye has gotten used to the dark. When I look at Elroy all I see is my cap above a pale face with smooth features. The collar of his jacket is still flipped up and if you had never heard his voice, you'd swear you were sitting next to a stocky sixteen-year-old kid.

"I'm sorry about your eye, Allen. I did not mean to close it up like that."

"Whatever."

"You asked me about my family. Why?"

"I saw a picture when I was packing your things. When was it taken?"

His weight shifts in the seat. I see him raise his beer and drink from it a long time before he lowers it. "Summer of 'sixty-six." He belches and I think how in 1966 I was eight years old and still had a mother.

"That was the last of the good years. Before the proverbial shit hit the fan, you could say."

"Where's your wife?"

"Living with a fat-ass car dealer in Gulfport, Mississippi."

"Oh."

He finishes his third beer and goes for his fourth. It's gotten cold in the car. I can hear the wind whistling past my radio antenna outside. Dry snow swirls against the windshield then settles on the wipers.

"Do you have a girl, Allen?"

"No."

"Don't you like girls?"

I think of that porno magazine back in Elroy's gear bag. "Nice ones."

"You ever been in love?"

I shrug my shoulders in the dark.

"Jimmy had a girl when he was your age. No. He was younger."

"Is he in Mississippi, too?"

Elroy begins to burp but then covers his mouth. He is absolutely still and quiet. Then he rests his cupped hand on the steering wheel. "Jim had a girl named Maura. Boy she loved him, too. She'd come down to the house every time she got a letter from him and she'd read it to us. All but the personal parts. *Damn,* she loved him."

"What are you talking about?"

"My boy Jimmy." He bottoms up his beer, drops the empty onto the backseat, and opens another. "You see, Al, my eight-year experiment with self-sufficiency just did not pan out. Man, I went from herbs to corn to chickens and eggs, with part-time building jobs the whole time—most times all five. But all that work just wasn't enough for those striped-tied motherfuckers down at the bank, nossir." He stops talking and looks straight ahead at the thin layer of snow covering the windshield. He drinks again and I'm thinking how cold my body is and how I don't give a shit about his failed farming ventures.

"The week we lost everything was blisterin' hot. I mean it was *hot.* It was June of 1970 and you would not believe the timing of it, Allen. It was the Lord's blackest hour, I'm telling you." He swallows more beer and I lay my head back against the seat and close my eye.

"It was Monday and I was halfway through my morning

chores when this young man from Rocky Mountain Bank came down to the house. He sat awhile and had coffee and pie, made small talk, you know. Then the sonuvabitch got up and politely left us a form letter on how to partially liquidate our property and avoid foreclosure by the bank. After he left, why Lorraine and I just stared at that piece of paper like it was a rattlesnake somebody'd dropped in our bed. That was Monday. Two days later my wife and I are finishing a fried-chicken lunch and that letter is still on the table where it was left. Then—and you are not goin' to believe this, Allen—then, a knock came on the screen door in the front. I got up first, hoping it might be that young sonuvabitch come to say he left the papers at the wrong house. But it wasn't. I knew what it was in seconds, though. I mean my world stopped when I saw that army captain with the chaplain's cross pinned on him. He said that there'd been an unfortunate error in communications and my deepest condolences, sir, but your son's body has been stateside for a week. He was down at Fort Carson." Elroy stops talking. The wind is really pushing outside. I want to ask him to turn on the engine and the heat, but I don't. I'm seeing that picture of his kid and wife in my head. I'm seeing the boy with the blond hair and Elroy's Cro-Magnon forehead, his somewhat happy face.

"Lorraine and I got in my pickup to go fetch him, and Lord, she was wailing. God, it was more than I could stand. We had the windows down the whole way, and do you know what I thought as I drove down that highway to get what was left of my boy? Lorraine cryin' beside me like somebody had stuck her with a knife? I thought: When did it happen? Lord, when did I die? Because the wind off the road was hot as fire and my wife was a screaming demon and I knew sure as shit that I had died in my sleep and gone straight to hell. At the gate they were very nice, two young corporals, and they had Lorraine go in the air-conditioned Officers' Quarters. Then a young E-3 got into my truck and directed me to a big hangar. And man, that concrete was so blindin' bright I didn't believe any of it was real. And you know? It wasn't. Not like any of the real your average man has ever lived. We drove into the hangar and turned off the ignition and, for a second, my eyes couldn't adjust to the dark of the place. Then while I was standing and leaning against my truck, and trying to get used to the light, a man came over and said: 'Name?' And I said, 'McElroy.' By this time my eyes had adjusted to the place and, by God, I couldn't believe what they were seeing. I was looking at fifty or sixty of those gray metal coffins lined against both walls like lumber in a lumber yard, and this man, who was some kind of a sergeant, was flipping through the names of dead boys on his clipboard. He said, 'McElroy, James A.' Then he handed his list to the E-3, who got into a forklift with it and drove off. Now Jesus, my knees were about to give way and I had to lean against the hood of my truck. I watched that machine drive along that awful row of boxes 'til it stopped. Well, that's when I had to turn my head. I looked outside over the concrete to the security gate and Officers' Quarters beside it. When I turned back around that sonuvabitch was coming at me with my Jimmy's coffin. When he swung around to the back of my pickup he stopped and said: 'Please lower your tailgate, sir.' I did this. Then he lowered that thing into the bed of my truck and I watched it go down, and I looked at that E-3 and saw him chewing gum. He was looking just as *bored* as could be. He wanted to finish this detail and go fuck his *girl*. The last few inches he let it drop, and that is when I lost it, Allen. I tore after that sonuvabitch like a bulldog. I got in about four good punches when that clipboard sergeant jerked me from behind. Well, that is the last thing he ever did, kid, because I pushed him outside and got on top of him and knocked his head into the concrete until he was no more. I mean to say I *killed* him. I never saw my boy's funeral either. The Honorable Judge Barton didn't think I deserved it. His exact words, too. 'You've lost that privilege,' he said."

"Jesus."

"Yep."

"Elroy, I—"

"It was an election year, too. And that old judge wasn't about to appear soft on a man who kills soldiers who are getting killed enough as it is. Never mind the fact that one of them was my boy. Don't mind *that*. He gave me the full twenty."

We are quiet. The radio antenna makes a long low ringing sound as the wind hits it in just the right place, but I can't see it. The snow on the windshield must be a good half inch deep. My nose is stopped up. My eye feels full of something, too. I can no longer feel my fingers and toes. I don't know if it's from the cold or from the rope. I don't know anything right now. "Could you turn on the heat, please?"

Elroy starts the engine and the heat. He turns on the headlights then flicks on the wipers. They move slowly, but push away the snow. It's coming down in swirls in front of the headlights. I see a fresh layer of it on the snowbank in front of us.

"Could you loosen the rope on my hands and feet, Elroy? I think they're going to fall off."

He looks at me, and in the light I see his eyes glisten. God. He even cries without a sound. He sniffles, wipes his nose on his sleeve, then pulls the Bowie from the inside lining of his jacket, leans over, and cuts all the way through the rope around my wrists. When it falls free he sits back and I open and shut my hands. I wince at the pain-tingle of them coming alive again. They feel as swollen as my eye, as stopped up as my nose. I am not in good shape.

"A fair pound of your flesh is all I ask, sir."

I look quickly at Elroy. He is holding the handle of the knife between his clasped palms, the blade sticking straight up past his fingers.

"What?"

"The flesh of the man who owes me. It's a play, Allen. *The Merchant of Venice*. I even acted the entire role of Shylock once. Ah, but I have forgotten that, too. Those were my cultured days in Greeley, kid. Those were days of suspended disbelief. What some fools call faith." Elroy rests his Bowie in his lap. I look at my watch; it's ten-seventeen, but this fact gives me no bearing. It could be morning or night, weekday or weekend, I don't know. I have only felt this way once before, when your whole constitution just goes liquid and will take on any shape that wants it. I want to reach over and touch Elroy's shoulder, tell him I know how gutted and ripped open he feels. But I don't move. I look straight ahead at the windshield wipers pushing away the snow as it falls, see the snowbank in front of us. I smell exhaust and imagine dying in this car with buzzed and deathly sad Douglas Agnes McElroy. I think of my brother, Mark, and his pretty, plump wife, Anne. I can't imagine that they're living life as usual in their condominium park just outside of Denver. I can't imagine that they don't know things aren't so good with me right now. And Leon. He's working the night shift waiting for Wilson so he can make it down to The Rhino before last call. Do they really not know that I am stuck in my car in Wyoming with escapee McElroy? Do they really not know that my eye is closed up from where he punched me? That my legs are tied? That he has the biggest knife I have ever seen and is getting drunk and morose and now, shit, unpredictable?

"Will you help me get to Saskatchewan, Allen?"

"I thought I was."

"I don't want to *make* you do it anymore." Elroy's voice just got as high and wavering as an old man's—full of phlegm. "I am tired of hitting my head against the wall."

"Let's go back, then."

"Nope." He clears his throat, rolls down the window, and spits outside. "No, kid. We are not going back. I am never going back. I am driving to Saskatchewan. It is there or dust for me. I am through with your Fascist House and every other manner of institution, for that matter. Never mind the eleven years of *my* life. For*get* that. I gave my boy to this land." With that last word, he picks the knife up out of his lap, clutches the handle, then stabs the point into the soft of my dashboard. He pushes all the way in, sliding the blade under the vinyl until I can see only the handle. He wipes his nose and sits up straight. We are both still, looking through the windshield together like something out there might have an answer for all of this. I look at Elroy behind the wheel and think of his black hair and smiling face in that oval portrait. I smell beer, then actually turn to reach for one, when Elroy snaps out of his trance and bangs the steering wheel with the palms of his hands. "God damn, Allen. Our time has come."

He puts the car in gear then jerks forward towards the snowbank. He gets her in reverse then pulls around the utility station and out into the road. He brakes and the wheels lock and we slide in the dark. Then we're driving back through the residential neighborhood, all lit up with discount-store electric cheer, heading for the 7-Eleven and, I think, a felony. I have never felt more gray about anything in my life. I almost want to nudge him and shout, "Not yet, Elroy. The store will be open for two more hours." But I stop myself. The road is soft with snow beneath us and we're gliding over it fast, too fast. I'm so nervous my left eye opens. It pulls apart sticky then burns. My right eye fills up and I wipe it dry as we hit the road between the Christmas houses and the 7-Eleven. There's one car parked in front of the store, the same one that was there two hours ago, the fat lady's. Elroy swerves into the parking lot and we do a half doughnut then slide and come to rest parallel to the curb in front of the place.

"A pound, a pound. A pound of Saskatchewownd," Elroy says in a voice both raspy and clear. He opens the door, pulls the knife out of my dash, belches, then turns to me in the light of my car. He's breathing fast, like we just ran here. "You can do it if you like, Allen. There's no feeling like it." He looks through the windshield at the store. "Has she seen us?"

"She's looking right at us."

"Then it's now or never." He smiles, pats me on the leg, and in seconds, is inside the store. There is a hot-coffee sign taped to the window in front of the counter and I have to lower my head close to the dashboard to see. My heart is beating very fast. McElroy is standing at the counter with my cap on his head and his dungaree jacket buttoned up to his throat, his collars flipped up like Elvis. He's got his hands behind his back and is smiling red-faced like he is embarrassed but excited too, like the woman behind the counter is looking at a part of him he didn't ask for but can't do anything about either. I can't see the fat lady's head because of the sign in the window, but she is standing up facing Elroy and her polyester pea green turtleneck is sticking with static to her belly. Then

McElroy moves very quickly and has his rough hand on her shoulder and is holding his huge Bowie knife an inch from her stomach. I see her plump fingers as her body turns towards the register. They have rings on them, lots of them, and I know that one of them is a wedding ring. I think I am going to throw up. I open my door and start to get out but my legs stay hugged together and I fall on my side and bang my head on the snowy concrete. I pull myself up until I am standing, holding on to the roof of my car, and I start to hop towards the glass door. "You're not going to do this, Elroy! You're not going to do this!" I make it to the curb and reach for the door's handle, when I see Elroy backing away from the counter. He has his hands and knife up in the air beside him and he is talking and smiling. I swing open the door then see her and the raised pistol, then hear it go *thack, thack, thack;* but I don't see it anymore because I am looking at Elroy as he takes one in his right shoulder, then twists and hunches as he gets one in the neck, then lunges sideways into a shelf as he catches the last in his back. His Bowie hits the floor before he does and clatters and spins down the aisle towards the coolers. Then the fat lady, pale as death, points her trembling gun at me. I jerk my hands over my head. *"I'm not with him. I'm his hostage. I'm not with him."* She keeps that pistol pointed at me and I see her chin start to quiver. I point at my feet. *"Look. He tied me up. Look at my face. He did this."* She lowers her gun, then sits down on her TV chair. "Oh, my Jesus," she says. "Oh, my holy Jesus."

I looked at Elroy curled up against the shelf on the floor. My cap is sitting way back on his head and his eyes are closed. There's a small hole just under the jaw and blood is leaving it in a pulsing, peaceful trickle. I hear the fat woman weeping. I let go of the door, lean back against it, and close my eye.

3

The officers from the Platte County Police Department were very nice; they patched up my eye and after I spent an hour and a half writing reports with them, they offered to put me up for the night in a hotel. But I turned them down. I'm just too keyed up to sleep. I pass a car on my right then get into the traveling lane. The highway is wet and slick but clear of snow. It's still coming down, but not nearly as hard. I touch my cheek under my left eye and feel the sticky stuff left over from the adhesive tape and gauze. I got rid of all that as I left the station, and I alternate holding my left eye open and keeping it closed. Right now it's closed and the eighteen wheeler in front of me looks like it could be two car lengths ahead of me, or six. I look at my watch, one thirty-two A.M. Twenty-four hours ago almost to the minute, I was lugging McElroy's things down to the tomb of the center: his radical books and immaculate work clothes, the picture of his dead son and runaway wife.

In the passing lane I leave the semi behind me, rub the slit in the upholstery of my dash, and hear what my brother, Mark, will say about all of this: "We'll throw everything at him, Alley. We'll put that fucker back behind the walls forever." I think of that fat woman after she pulled the trigger three times and watched what the kick and blast in her hands could do to a man. There was no color in her face at all; her flesh got as white and lifeless-looking as bread dough. Then she slumped in her stool and covered her face with the hands that had done it, that had known more power in a few seconds than she had probably ever imagined. I have never seen anyone shot before. A man's body doesn't take them straight and unflinching like a silhouetted target. I wonder if the beer in Elroy's belly gave him any relief at all. I doubt it.

I drive and drive and think of nothing. At three thirty-four A.M., I pass to the west of Cheyenne. The streets and some of the buildings are still lit up. And the sidewalks are dusted with snow, no footprints on them yet. At four oh-two A.M. I cross the state line into Colorado. The road is dry in front of me, no fresh snow anywhere. When I get into Bellington I pull into Winchell's and buy two chocolate eclairs and a large coffee with a little cream, no sugar. There are no customers and the girl behind the counter looks young, around seventeen. When she takes my money she looks up at my face.

"Wow. The other guy looks worse, I hope."

"I'm afraid so."

"Good. Have a nice night."

"You, too." I take my bag and as I'm leaving, I think how wrong it is for a girl that age to be watching a cash register at this time of the night. Then I imagine a big .45, or a long .357, or a short and flat .380 semiautomatic probably sitting under the counter to back her up. I get back on the road and eat my eclairs all at once. If my father had been working at the 7-Eleven in Wyoming last night, what would he have done? Would he have gone for Elroy's vital-organ zones? Or would he have aimed for his elbows and knees and shoulders?

Just before Longmont I finish my coffee and decide to take 119 southwest to Boulder instead of continuing straight on down into Denver and my apartment. This thing with Elroy's going to take a long report. I'd just as soon get it done with now. I open my left eye as I go through a blinking yellow traffic light in the center of Longmont, then close it as I hit the rushing yellow lines of 119 heading towards Niwot. There is snow on both sides of the road, old snow. I run my fingers through my hair then miss something and know it's my wool cap. I remember the way it looked on Elroy as he lay bleeding, curled up and still. It was almost jolted off him, but then stayed, sitting on the back of his unconscious head as pointed and idiotic-looking as a party hat.

When I drive through Niwot I see the Sunoco station up ahead and I open my left eye to that same kid sitting in the lighted office leaning back in his chair reading a magazine. That's what Wilson's doing right now I know, reading when he should be outside doing a perimeter check before daybreak, walking around the center, cold or not, shining his flashlight up under window ledges, looking for nickel bags on a string.

At five thirty-six in the morning I drive into Boulder. The street-lights are almost blue in this town, and as I pass the park on my left, I look at the way that light looks natural when cast upon the snow. Muddy River Johnson died in that park, and I think how Elroy's and Muddy River's gear share the same space in the base-ment at the center; but Johnson's dead and Elroy is lying in a hos-pital in Wyoming with three .38-caliber holes in him. I pass The Rhino, then the mall and Rocky Mountain Bank on my right. I see the green glimmer of the electric-eye alarm system cast over the floor of the bank's lobby. When I get to Broadway I stop, put on my indicator, then take a left up the street. My heart flutters a sec-ond in my chest, stops, then flutters again. I feel very strange. Not tired really, but past tired, not fully in my body. At the top of the hill, a dairy truck is pulled up to the side of Pau-Pau's Variety Store. The driver is wearing a hat and gloves and a thick-looking coat and is unloading full milk crates into the light of the store. He doesn't notice me or my Monte Carlo as I turn right and drive past him onto University down through fraternity row. Over the roofs of the big houses are the white rise and dip of the foothills. I look in the direction of the French restaurant but only see the steep icy face of Dead Goat Ridge.

I turn into the alley in the back of the center, park behind Wilson's motorcycle, turn off my engine and lights, and just sit here. There's the faint buzzing of someone's alarm clock going off. I look out my windshield up at the darkened windows of the men's wing and see one of them wide open: Buck's. I imagine his three-hundred-and-thirty-two-pound body waking up to piss and wash, then dress and put on his forty-pound custom made Satan's Siblings leather jacket that he keeps draped over a chair beneath the window. I think of Bill Paxton's snoring face doing subtle brain damage to Glenn Peters and Russ Haywood. And I imagine Maggie Nickerson waking up then walking to the women's rest room with her blue sleeping cap pulled tightly over her scalp, her old face still puffy with sleep. I think of these people and I wish Leon was working now. Then after I finished writing my report, he and I could go down to the Montview Hotel for breakfast, order blueberry pancakes and syrup with three eggs over easy and two double orders of bacon with lots of hot coffee. We'd sit and eat, and in between bites I'd tell him all about my night with Elroy. Leon's face would get very serious and he'd stop chewing when I'd tell him about Elroy's son. Then he'd shake his head and tell me I'd better go home and rest and put ice over my eye. We leave the waitress a big tip, then walk to our separate cars and make plans to get together for a few beers at The Rhino later on. I would get into my Monte Carlo and leave Boulder heading east towards Denver and my apartment, electric blanket, and bed. I would be driving, wired as all hell, but I would see Elroy looking over that shimmering stretch of concrete to the air-conditioned Officers' Quarters for his wife, then turning to see his son's coffin coming at him then being dumped into his pickup truck like a load of bricks, then him going after the kid and the clipboard sergeant grabbing Elroy from behind, and Elroy slamming the guy's head against concrete until he was dead and Elroy wasn't just Elroy anymore, but a murderer.

When the EMTs strapped him into the gurney I opened my left eye, sticky burn or not, and looked down at his face. His eyes were closed and his cheeks were the color of oatmeal. There was a big spot of blood coming through the sheet near his neck, and even his eyebrows looked a little less bushy, but I knew he wasn't slipping away; he was simply being silent. Like when he sleeps, and cries. He was lying low when vulnerable, not about to let another creature hear him then get him in the night.

I get out of my car and close the door. I start to lock it but then stop when I remember the popped lock on the passenger's side. I walk around the center just in time to see the streetlamp go off on the corner of Tenth Avenue. The dawn sky is vast and gray and what little light there is looks like it might be coming more from the snow on the ground. I walk to the side door and unclip my keys, look through the glass down at the mess hall that is partly lighted from the kitchen. I can barely see the Christmas tree in the corner. I find the right key, work it in the lock, and pull the door open. But the handle is metal, and sticks to my fingers like the bottom of an ice cube tray.

DUCKLING GIRL

In a Salvation Army box in El Cerrito Lorilee Waters dreams her face and head are huge, but they keep growing and growing and are getting so big now that they hurt; she opens her eyes fast like somebody just called her name and when she sees rust streaks on the dark green sheet metal above her, a ray of daylight coming in at the wall near her head, she knows right away where she is and so touches her face, pushes lightly on the puffy part where the bones underneath feel like they are being stung by a bee.

"You dumb ugly bitch. You ugly fucking whore," he had kept saying, nothing else, and it had lasted so much longer than the other times, and he never let go. In the dark Lorilee can see the

thin white threads of a spider's web in the corner, then his face, red and more bloated than normal, his eyes all shiny and mean-looking. But Papa was drinking, she thinks, her skin and eyes remembering his fist gripping the hair at the side of her head, jerking on it while he yelled about things Lorilee didn't understand or even hear when the hot light flashed through her head. Then he kicked her shins and she'd bent her knees to the kitchen floor, had smelled the beer on his favorite shirt that was stretched tight over his big belly. She had said, "Okay, you can stop now, okay," before she had let go of his fist then unzipped his pants, reached in and grabbed that thing that she knew would soon empty itself inside her, would make him loosen his grip on her hair. But then he bent her over the TV and was pushing into the wrong place, cutting into her with his fatty hardness.

Lorilee hears the steel choke and mesh of something big coasting to change gears outside. She pulls the damp-smelling wool coat off of her then licks a sweat drop from her upper lip. He had been asleep when she slowly, so slowly, slid out from under his heavy arm, got off the couch, then walked naked into the bathroom and sat on the toilet. Then she was dressed, and just before she crept through the kitchen then out the door into the night, she had looked down at his sleeping bulk on the couch, had seen in the TV's flickering blue light the peace in his face, in his closed eyes and slightly opened snoring mouth. And she had felt nothing but that hot stomach-turning hate for the power she knew she would always have but lately could not control.

See. Something bad happens, Lorilee thinks as she crawls over the huge pile of clothes away from the smell of pennies and wet sneakers toward the light. Something always happens. She slides back the metal door then climbs out of the steel box into the brightness of the day, blinking at it. She tastes her spit and wishes for a toothbrush then pulls her long stringy blond hair back out of her face and tucks it behind her ears. And with a sore ache living now in the exact center of her body she walks down San Pablo Street, walks with the sun hot on her head, a queasiness growing in her stomach.

FREEZE LOOKS AT THE plum-purple bruise on Lorilee's cheek, blue-black around the edges. "Check it out. Who you been playing with?"

"Nobody." She moves over the front seat and sits beside him. "My dad was mad 'cause I forgot to make his lunch."

"Can't fuck with a man's stomach," Barry says. He gets in beside her and pulls the door shut, looks down at her big breasts pushing against the white material of her shirt. When Freeze pulls back onto San Pablo Barry takes another sip from his bottle of Mateus.

Freeze drives fast through El Cerrito into Richmond and all the windows are down but the inside of the car is so hot Lorilee smells the old vinyl of the seats, the rust of the ceiling under its tattered covering, a hanging flap of it rippling back against itself. They pass the small shops and pool halls along San Pablo, some with windows held together with dusty gray plumber's tape, this one-story row of wood and cinder-block buildings looking as settled in their shabbiness as the old men who sit in the shadows of the stoops.

"We're going up to the quarry," Barry says to Lorilee. "The beach is too friggin' hot and crowded." He takes the bottle from her and wipes it before drinking. When he hands it over to Freeze his arm pushes against Lorilee's breasts. Her cheeks flush, and when they do, pain breathes heavy under her eye. She reaches up to tilt the mirror down but then Freeze's hand slaps hers away.

"Do you guys have any aspirin I could take?"

Barry is tapping his fingers hard on the dashboard in time to the Tom Petty tape Freeze has been playing all morning. He looks at Lorilee looking back at him then shakes his head in time to the beat, looks straight ahead again.

"Here." Freeze takes another sip then wedges the bottle down between Lorilee's closed legs. It feels cool and damp there and Lorilee waits a second or two before picking it up. Freeze pulls the car up over the gravel and parks it under the jackknife-scarred branches of the old tree. They overlook the pit of the quarry.

"All right. Nobody's here," Barry says as they get out of the car. Freeze keeps the music going and walks around to the front, sits on the hood in the shade. He looks out over the muddy water that is almost green in the midday sun, and lights a cigarette. "How's Glenn?"

"What?" Lorilee turns away from Barry, stripped to his skivvies, toe-stepping over the gravel down the slope to the water. She sits on the hood beside Freeze.

"What did you say?"

"How's your brother Glennie doing?"

Lorilee shrugs her shoulders. "Who knows? Do you have an extra cigarette, Freeze?"

He offers her his pack, watches her take one then put it to her lips. He hands her his cigarette and she lights hers with it. They both hear Barry's flabby body make a big splash.

"I think he's on a ship. He sent a postcard with a picture of a big ship on it."

Lorilee takes a deep drag off her cigarette, remembers the slow sway of her brother's chain bracelet over the green felt, the crack of the break, the balls rolling out in every direction on the table, then the thunk of one falling into a corner pocket. He had looked up at her with his fist-swollen lips. *"The marines, man. Fuck him. I don't have to eat his shit anymore."*

Freeze looks at Lorilee's face. "Get the bottle out of the car, will ya?"

"Okay."

Freeze sees Barry's whiteness splashing in the water below.

"Come on in, man. Nothin' like it."

"Later."

Lorilee leans into the music to pick the bottle up off the front seat and when she straightens brown fills her eyes; she half sits, half drops to the seat, breathes deeply through her nose, and looks straight ahead at the gravel, at bits of broken glass that glitter there in the sun.

"Where's the wine?"

Lorilee stands back up and walks around the open door to the front of the car and Freeze. She hands him the bottle, picks her burning cigarette up off the hood, and leans against the grille. It hurts the most when she sits, a pain she has only known once before when her bowels were heavy but she had to wait for her father to come out of the bathroom first, when it seemed that hours passed before she heard the toilet flush and saw the door open. It had felt like a steel chain being pulled from her insides and there was blood and she had to lie down after.

Freeze nudges her arm with the bottle, wipes his mouth with the back of his hand. Lorilee looks at it; she wants a Coke and a sandwich, maybe two. She takes the bottle and sips from it.

"How's your face?"

"I have a headache."

"Your old man's a fucking asshole, you know that, don't you?"

"Yeah."

"So move."

"I can't."

"Why?" Freeze slides off the hood.

"I never worked before."

"You can work at a fuckin' hamburger place."

"I can't do the applications, Freeze."

"Jesus." Freeze picks up a handful of gravel, weighs it in his hand, then throws all of it under the branches of the tree and out over the pit at Barry swimming on his back; they rip into the water around him like shrapnel.

"Hey!"

"Air attack, General. What can I say?"

"*Fuck you,* man."

Lorilee sees Barry treading water, his shaved head glistening under the sun looking as black-nubbed and pink-white as a puppy's belly.

"You could've put an eye out."

"Then you'd really look like a killer."

Freeze turns to Lorilee, his face looking younger to her; she looks between the opening of his sleeveless denim jacket, sees the smooth skin of his chest, the neat divided sections of his stomach muscles.

"He's an asshole," Freeze says. He looks straight into her eyes then down at her mouth. "Everybody's an asshole."

"Not everybody." Lorilee flicks her cigarette away then feels it, the sudden flesh awareness of all the openings of her body where shadows have formed and now lie and wait, her tissues preparing themselves without her permission, and she knows that when her eyes meet his she will end up saying and doing whatever he wants. Freeze picks up more gravel then paces with it, looking to Lorilee like somebody with something stolen in his hand and no place to hide it. She looks at the way he can't seem to stop moving, thinks, Something's wrong with you, Freeze Benito.

He drops one pebble at a time from his closed fist then drops all of it, steps toward her. He looks from her mouth to her blue eyes then takes her hand and presses it down between his legs. "Let's go behind the rock."

With her eyes closed against the sun her head aches less but she is sweating very much and it is beginning to burn the swollen side of her face. "C'mon, Freeze, c'mon." She reaches down and pulls on his cheeks. "C'mon, baby." She is beginning to chafe. She smells the coconut oil Freeze puts in his hair to slick it back, then feels cool drops of water land on her forehead and closed eyes.

"What about me?"

Lorilee opens her eyes to Barry's white hairless belly, his upside-down smiling face.

"Get the fuck outta here, man. I'm almost done."

Lorilee closes her eyes again and Freeze moves faster, pushes harder then stops, pushes once more then stops again, relaxes his weight on her. She scratches the back of his neck with her fingers. "Did you like it?"

"Yeah, sure."

She moves her mouth to his cheek but he sees her and pulls out fast, is up zipping and snapping his pants, stepping over her.

"Go for it," Freeze says.

Lorilee blocks the sun from her eyes with her hand, sees Barry still in his underpants holding the bottle of wine. His round face looks at hers then he glances between her legs, places the bottle on the rock, and pulls down his underwear.

Lorilee sits up.

"What's the matter?"

"I have to wait."

"Why?"

"I just do."

"You want some wine?"

"No."

"Well then fuckin' blow me or somethin'."

Lorilee looks up past the dark hair and rising penis to his face.

"Come on." Barry pulls her head to his middle and with shadows wavering over her tongue and behind her teeth, Lorilee closes her eyes to make them leave, opens her mouth to Barry's ugliness, her head falling into a rhythm that pulses now through her hollow stomach, behind her closed and aching eyes. He pushes rough and deep. She works harder but they are not leaving, inner pockets of heat that can't be rubbed away, and their voices have come too; Freeze's and Barry's and Papa's and now Glennie's, who touched her mouth with his fingers once and said, *"Don't smile when you're not happy, Lore. It don't help nothing."*

Barry grunts and she grips the tremble in his legs then finishes it, opens her eyes again to the light, to Barry backing up, hopping one-footed into his wet underpants over the gravel and parched grass.

At the car, Lorilee opens the front door at the passenger side.

"In the back," Freeze says.

"I'm sorry." In the backseat Lorilee is sweating and when Freeze rewinds the tape then turns it up her head aches more than ever. "Freeze?"

"What?"

"Do you think maybe we could get some food?"

Barry gets in the car and looks over his shoulder at Lorilee. "You have money?"

"No."

"Well then."

Freeze laughs and then Barry does too, shaking his shaved head back and forth. He bends over to tie his sneakers as Freeze backs the car up fast over gravel. When he gets it turned around, Lorilee looks out the window down at the sun on the water in the quarry, wishes she had at least waded in and splashed the good part of her face.

Freeze drives fast into El Cerrito. They stop at Kentucky Fried Chicken then are driving again, Barry handing the coleslaw back to Lorilee, she passing the plastic containers of gravy and mashed potatoes up to him.

"Have some chicken, paisan," Barry says to Freeze.

"Don't want it."

Barry tosses a roll into Freeze's lap. "Here."

Freeze picks it up and drops it out the window. "Junk." He looks in the rearview mirror at Lorilee. She is chewing carefully, the wind blowing her thin blond hair out of her bruised face. "I wouldn't eat after her if you *paid* me."

Lorilee stops chewing; she looks at the back of Freeze's head then swallows and looks back out the window.

"Whatever," Barry says. He reaches into the grease-spotted cardboard box for another piece of chicken.

Freeze takes them up a hill where there are large brown and yellow painted houses with wide yards of shaded green grass, the trees tall enough to shade the houses too. Lorilee looks through the back window and can see the bay out there below them: white clouds have covered the bridge and moved in on the city. She sees the tops of buildings sticking out of the fog catching the sun in their tiny square windows. Then they're in darkness passing through a tunnel made of heavy square bricks covered with orange and green painted words Lorilee can't understand. They come out again into the day and Freeze slows down as they move into Berkeley.

"I don't get it, Freeze," Barry says. "Why'd your mother send you a hundred bucks?"

"How the fuck do *I* know?"

"Hey, I'm sorry, all right? Jesus."

"I don't know. Maybe the bitch is feeling guilty." Freeze looks over at Barry. "Let's go blow it."

"Now you're talkin', bud." Barry opens his mouth long for a bullhorn of a burp.

Freeze turns right onto Telegraph. The street is narrow but the sidewalks are wide, shaded by trees that look to Lorilee like they were built there just like all the different shops with windows full of clothes and stereos and hanging green plants. She looks out at two women on the sidewalk sitting on a jewelry-covered blue blanket under a tree. One has long braided hair that hangs down in front of her and they are both barefoot, the bottoms of their feet black with dirt.

She leans her head back against the seat and tries to ignore the electric scream and thump of the music coming from each side of her head. People are looking at them as they drive by and Lorilee wishes Freeze would turn it down. She can't remember ever coming here before, to this place full of so many different-looking kinds of people, and so she watches them, sees in the darkened doorway of a building a blind man picking the strings of his metal guitar, his eyes hidden behind glasses covered with grimy masking tape, his brown cheeks sucking in past the bones of his face. She looks away to the other side of the street where two bald men wearing long orange robes are singing and swaying, one of them shaking and tapping a tambourine.

"Hey, you want to watch where you're goin'," Barry says, lightly slapping Freeze's shoulder with the back of his hand. Freeze brakes the car for two women dressed in white tennis clothes, their legs long and tan and smooth-looking.

"All right, *babies!*" Barry says, sticking his head out the window. The two women turn to the car smiling, then turn back around and walk faster to the other side of the street.

"College chicks," Freeze says. "Their faces are always on fuckin' automatic pilot."

Lorilee looks after them as Freeze speeds up, thinks of her own white thighs, which are sweating now under her jeans. She feels better after the food, is no longer afraid that if she moves too fast her brain will float up and tap at the inside of her skull just before she blacks out, but still there are the dark places that are not going away; usually they do.

When she is on her hands and knees scrubbing the carpet in the hall of her father's apartment building, the sweat breaking out under her clothes like a warm thin oil to move better by, the shadows and voices that make her body feel like the home of other people become small, seem to go to sleep inside her; when she is opening a can of peas or shaking salt and pepper over a tuna and potato chip casserole after having just cleaned the whole apartment, sipping a diet Pepsi, they are quiet. Sometimes she has thought about it and wondered if it is the work that makes them that way, or is it being alone that does it? For they always come alive when she is not alone, when men look at and talk to her and she has to look and talk back. Any kind of man.

Whenever she walks down to the 7-Eleven for cigarettes or for her father's beer, she tries not to look into the eyes of skinny Clifford standing behind the counter. Once he pointed to the plastic name tag on his chest and told her his name and he always wants to talk, standing there in his orange-and-white checkered shirt. But things begin to happen inside her when she can't leave right away; warm spots twitch and breathe, stretch, then come alive in her mouth and down between her legs, inside the crack of her bottom. Like uninvited guests moving to let in more, they make her face grow hot. She leaves as soon as his hand drops the change into hers, not once looking up past the moving Adam's apple of his too-white throat, and as she walks out into the parking lot she thinks he thinks, and all of them think, it's because she's embarrassed about her looks.

But then she can be curled up alone almost asleep and they will just be there; it will get bright in her head and she will see and hear them behind her eyes just before her bones relive their weight, her flesh their entry. She will sit up and light a cigarette in the dark. Drawing deep on it, she'll rock back and forth on the bed. At first they will tingle and there will be loud whispers. Then their voices will come sharp and clear, swimming through her like electric heat, and they will start to fill her. Sometimes she will feel like spitting as she tastes their juices again and she will have to stand up and pace in her panties over the linoleum floor of her room, all of them becoming one inside her so that she is not she at all but them, until it feels as if she has never been her but just a part of them that they have kept in their lives for whenever they needed to let things out, a dark and evil part.

Then, as sudden as summer rain comes after the smell of hot street dirt in the air, they stop. She will put out her cigarette, lie back down in a sweat she can smell, then wait for her heart and stomach and breathing to slow down enough for sleep or the first gray light of day.

But things are yawning and squirming now so Lorilee moves over the seat to the window behind Barry. The pain is sharper now beneath her and she wonders vaguely if the dampness she feels there is from Freeze or is it blood? She looks away from the people of the street moving by to the two who she knows have got it now, the sickness; Freeze has put on his dark sunglasses and has an unlit cigarette hanging out of the corner of his mouth, and Barry, his face halfway out the window, is moving his shaved head in time to the music, tapping the outside of the car with the palms of his hands and smiling, Lorilee thinks, like a crazy person whenever anybody looks his way. She wonders if they will get as mean and ugly as her father. No. This is real bad, she thinks, looking at the side of Barry's pudgy face staring out at everyone on the sidewalks, the bass of the rock and roll behind her reaching out and tapping at the back of her head, constant and teasing. She leans forward and folds her arms on the front seat, lays her cheek on them.

"Cooper still working that corner by the chink place?" Freeze asks Barry.

"Fuckin' *a*, Freeze. Now you're cookin', now you're fuckin' cookin', man." Barry reaches over and tousles Freeze's oiled hair. "Toot town here we *come*."

"Hands off." Freeze knocks Barry's arm with the back of his hand then reaches up to fix his hair.

"What is your *prob*lem?" Barry says. "We haven't had a day

like this in friggin' weeks. And you got a stick up your ass like we're busted or somethin'. I mean Jesus, enjoy it, huh?" Barry turns around to Lorilee. "Hey Waters, you ever do coke before?"

"Yes."

"*When?*" Freeze asks, turning his head to see her face near his shoulder.

"With Glennie."

"*With Glennie,*" Freeze says, raising the pitch of his voice. Barry laughs. Lorilee looks at him.

"Don't forget you owe me still," Barry says.

"What?" Lorilee asks then immediately wishes she hadn't.

"*What?*" Barry turns to Freeze then to Lorilee. "A hot fuck, bitch."

Freeze laughs so hard his cigarette falls out of his mouth into his lap. Barry laughs then turns around and knocks out a hard fast drum roll on the dash. "All *right.*"

THE DARK-SKINNED OLD MAN clears his throat in the backseat. "Here's good." Dave pulls the cab over in front of a brown two-story building, its porch sitting so crooked he imagines laying a basketball on it then watching it roll quickly down and out the broken-toothed railing into the weed and asphalt lot next door. The old man is out of the cab, unfolding with stubby fingers that shake slightly a five-dollar bill. Dave reaches his hand for it, thinks two-thirty after a two-seventy fare. He puts the five with the others, reaches for his coin belt then stops, counts out three one-dollar bills, and hands them to the old man standing outside in the sun.

"Gracias."

Dave watches him push the bills deep into the pocket of his flappy khaki pants then turn around slowly for the climb up the worn steps to the shade of his broken porch.

He is driving south on 57, the dead weed smell of the bay blowing hot at the side of his face. He picks at the chef's salad in the clear plastic container on the seat beside him and thinks maybe it's because he is polite and clean shaven that they don't stand and count it to make sure he has not short-changed them like some of the other cabbies do. Once a big white woman in a dirty peach cotton dress found the extra dollar and started to put her arm through the open window at the passenger side, but Dave pulled out fast and loud onto San Angelo. He looked up into his rearview mirror and saw her standing there open-mouthed, her arm outstretched, the dollar still in her hand.

Dave flips the visor down and gets in the right lane. He takes the Berkeley exit and looks over the guardrail at a black freighter out on the bay. He follows the curve left and crosses the overpass into the first shaded neighborhood of Berkeley. When he comes to Gardenia and Telegraph he slows almost to a stop then pulls into the intersection for the climb to Berkeley Hills. He looks to his left down the crowded narrow street to the white stucco walls of the university, sees all the people only two or three years younger than he walking on the sidewalks, some crossing the street with books or ice cream cones in their hands, others standing alone waiting for buses, and their faces hold that look he has only become aware of recently but now sees all the time; it is a look of complete confidence, not so much in themselves, Dave knows, but in their steadfast belief that the world owes them something for the trouble they are taking to become educated. He looks straight ahead again and presses on the gas pedal until he hears the engine of the old

Ford taxi straining against the hill. He turns right on Citadel Drive, parks in front of an empty space where there is nothing but sky then the tops of buildings poking out of the haze of San Francisco across the bay. He turns off the motor and looks out at the bright specks of sun on the water, sees that same freighter passing under the bridge now, its movement barely detectable, the long arrow-shaped wake behind it looking stationary too. He steps out of the car and walks to the edge of the overlook, shoves his hands into his pockets and feels the automatic flex of his triceps and upper back muscle. He looks down at the red slate rooftops of the Berkeley campus stretched out below, flat and bright in the sun, and the green fluff of trees that thins out as he looks westward and sees the wide expanse of the bay with its two long curving bridges. This spring he said no to his tennis-slender gray-haired father, and his offer to be a paid summer intern at the Baltimore office.

"I want to warm up to California over the summer, Dad."

"You haven't even gotten your letter of acceptance yet."

"I know."

"What about money? You know my policy there."

"I'll find something."

Dave walks to the open door of his cab, reaches in for his lunch. He sits on the hood, which is hot beneath him, and begins to eat then stops. He looks out over the bay to the thin blue lip of Pacific Ocean just beyond the city, and sees the letter to his father that he has not yet been able to write: the letter that will say *what?,* he asks himself, that I have no soft place in my heart for those men and women I pick up at the Hyatt and Sheraton here? That I cannot do what you do? Dad, I will not make the focus of my life's energy the designing of tax shelters for men who never have to worry about starving or freezing once they can no longer work; men who have not looked at and tried to help those who have to worry about such things. Yes, I'm still going to law school, don't worry about that. You can still refer to me as your lawyer son at parties, Dad. But I won't be working for the people you do.

TALL BLACK MARCUS COOPER takes Freeze's money then hands him the white packet. Freeze walks back down the narrow passage between the two restaurants, the smells of fish and french fries and fried rice hanging there, then ducks under a dripping air conditioner and comes out onto the sidewalk. Lorilee leans against the trunk of a slim tree, watching how he crosses the narrow one-way street without looking either way, his hand in his right jeans pocket, pressed flat over what that money has just bought him. He reaches her under the shade of the tree, and says: "Which one did he go in?"

"He's in there." She points to a small bottle-cluttered window set between two record and stereo stores. "Did you get what you wanted?"

Freeze nods his head then turns from her and puts his sunglasses back on, looks out at all the young people passing by. Lorilee watches how straight he is standing, his hair so dark and wet-looking; she wants to reach over and touch his face.

"Shit if it ain't Cruisin' Bruisin' Benito," Barry says, coming up from behind them and hugging Freeze with his free arm. Freeze spins away from him; smiling so his face looks frozen that way, he slaps Barry on each cheek with two hands like a boxer. "The deed is done, motherfucker. Let's *go.*"

Barry looks at Lorilee then grabs her by the wrist and pulls her after him. "C'mon. Don't you want to watch?"

They walk down the sidewalk, Lorilee in the middle, a step or two behind them. She keeps her head bowed low away from all the people's faces, wishes Freeze let her stay in the car or at least get some makeup to try and cover her cheek with. They step off the curb and walk across the street, Freeze and Barry taking their time, walking even slower when a small orange car brakes and the woman driving it honks her horn. Lorilee starts to walk ahead of them when she sees Freeze reach down and grab himself over his pants then push his hips out at the lady in the car.

Lorilee walks faster. She steps onto the sidewalk and ignores her reflection in the shoe store window as she hurries around the corner out into the open parking lot of Ameri-Bank. Oh no. She stops and stands there on the smooth black asphalt in the sun. She hears Freeze and Barry come up behind her and then stop too.

"Where's my car, man? Where the fuck's my car?" Freeze walks past her, his shoulder bumping hers. He looks down at the space he parked the Chevy in like he expects the faded yellow lines to tell him where it went.

"What the *fuck*." Barry walks past her too, stands next to Freeze.

"Look at this." Freeze points to a large square sign mounted on the white brick wall of the shoe store.

"The motherfuckers," Barry says. "Why don't they put 'em closer to the friggin' parking lot?"

Freeze turns and walks fast to the bank's green glass door, near the drive-in teller's window. Barry and Lorilee follow, Lorilee walking slow and guarded, the way she does whenever men start to shout. Freeze slams the glass with his open hand.

"Cock*suck*ers."

"What?"

"They closed at noon."

"Fuck, man." Barry steps closer to the building and pulls the bottle out of the bag, opens it and takes a big sip, then with his cheeks full, reaches back into the bag for the plastic container of Coke. He swallows the rum then chases it. "Nothin' we can do, buddy." Barry offers Freeze the bottle.

"The motherfuckers." Freeze takes the rum then drinks it until Lorilee sees two big air bubbles move up then pop in the bottom of the bottle pointing to the sky. Freeze lowers it fast to his side, his face spread tight. Barry holds out the bottle of Coke.

Freeze ignores him, looks to his left and right then at Lorilee. "What the fuck are you looking at? Get over here."

Lorilee walks into the shade of the building, stands next to Barry leaning against the drive-in teller window. Barry reaches over, grabs her buttocks, and squeezes.

"God*damn,*" Freeze says, lighting a cigarette.

"Paisan. We can't do shit about this 'til tomorrow so don't worry about it, all right?"

"*You* don't worry about it. I ain't got thirty something bucks."

"Waters'll lend it to us, won't you, Lore?" Barry puts his arm around Lorilee's shoulders, pulls her into his soft chest. "Won't you?"

Lorilee feels her face smile. She purses her lips over her teeth. "I don't have any money."

"No shit," Freeze says, handing the bottle over to Barry. "And if you could fucking read we'd be cruising with some tunes right now."

Barry begins to sip from the bottle then stops and holds it under Lorilee's flushed face. She lets him tilt it up then swallows until she coughs. Barry laughs, his face looking to Lorilee as smooth and plump as a clown's. Then he drinks and Lorilee puts her arm around his back, pulls herself in as close as she can.

"Freeze, baby," Barry says. "Let's just do the toot and then friggin' flow with it, all right?"

Lorilee looks at the way Freeze is drawing in on his cigarette like it's the last breath of air on earth.

"Yeah, fuck it." He drops the butt then steps on it. "Let's go."

LORILEE IS SITTING on the ground against the brick wall of the restaurant with her knees drawn up to her breasts watching Freeze divide the small pile of powder into thin straight lines on the glass. He is doing it with Barry's knife, his little pocket mirror resting on his Indian-crossed legs, and Barry is standing between the wall and the Dumpster looking at Freeze then back over his shoulder toward the metal-clanging, water-spraying sounds coming through the screen door of the kitchen. Freeze looks up at Barry.

"Chill out, General. Nobody in there gives a shit what we're doing."

"How do you know?" Barry drinks from the bottle of rum then the Coke.

Freeze holds his stare on Barry. "Because they're a bunch of wetback chinks, dummy. What the fuck are they gonna do?"

Barry turns a metal milk case on its side and sits against the Dumpster across from Lorilee. He looks at her face. "You look peek-ed."

Lorilee smiles and lowers her head, the shadow voices stretching like flatworms inside her, long and thin, twisting through her middle; they smile there in her dark. Barry holds the bottle to her.

Lorilee stands up and walks over to him then sits on the ground between his legs, her back against him. She takes the bottle dangling in front of her and drinks. She looks at Freeze lowering his nose to the tightly rolled one-dollar bill. She lays her head against Barry's soft belly, her arms resting on his legs, but she gets no peace from his stillness. She turns on her side and lays her ear on the hardness in his pants. Barry rests a hand on her head but they are not slowing down: *You fucking* dumb *ugly bitch.* And she smells her father's boozy yelling mouth spraying spit in her eye, on her nose and lips, and she thinks of men and women in white washing her in a bath she must stay in for days then giving her shots and more shots. She cannot remember it ever getting this bad, her flesh feeling so tender that very soon her body will split wide open with the whirling pus of all that she has done. She raises the bottle to her mouth again. Then she has moved and a smile pulls itself across her face. She is holding one nostril closed with her finger, trying to keep the rolled dollar steady in her hand, breathing in and making a snorting noise. Then she sits back against the wall and looks up at Freeze and Barry watching her, Barry smiling, his face looking so round, his head big and ugly with no hair. She looks at his face as if for the first time; she sees every faint wrinkle and line in his forehead, then a small white scar on his nose; and little indentations where flesh is stuck to bone, and pimples she has not noticed, and she imagines herself tiny enough to lie between the black nubs of whiskers, where oil lies on his pores. Naked, she would look out at the world holding on to the hair roots of his chin, fighting the slip of it with her feet. She begins to laugh, sees Barry's clown face laughing too, and she laughs so hard she is bent over, her breasts swaying and bobbing under her shirt. She raises her laughing head to see Freeze on his feet doing a dance with Barry's knife, the light blue veins coming out in his lean arms. He swings open the blade, letting it click against the air, then jabbing with it, his face reddening. Lorilee stops laughing when Freeze takes knife swipes at flies buzzing up and away from the Dumpster.

"Hiiiyuh." Freeze kicks his leg high in the air between them, then spins around, slashing the space his foot has vacated.

Barry laughs so hard Lorilee can see a vein come out on each side of his forehead leading into his skull. Freeze stands still. He holds the knife in his right fist at his side, his arm extended in front of him. He turns and narrows his eyes straight ahead at the brick wall above and behind Lorilee. "Ho go sho tau."

Lorilee hunches her shoulders slightly when Freeze's face lets go.

"Iiieeee-fuck." He snaps the knife forward in his right hand, pulling back his left.

Lorilee shrieks as Freeze squats in front of her, his eyes two dark slits. He rests his left arm against the wall then runs the flat of the blade cool along her cheek. "Don't fuck with Mastuh Fleeze, mama-san."

"Don't, Freeze."

Freeze lowers the blade to the soft of her upper lip, lets it rest there. "Call me mastuh, white bitch."

Lorilee feels the tickle of a tear as it rolls down over her swollen cheek. She presses the back of her head against the brick.

"Come on, High Master, you're scarin' the piss out of her."

Lorilee looks from Freeze's tight lips to his eyes, and just before his face spins away from hers, she sees in them the dark gaze of a child. He springs and spins out of his crouch, lands on his feet in front of smiling Barry who raises his hands, then turns his head to the slam of the screen door, to the short Oriental man in a white T-shirt who stops as soon as he sees them, a bulging plastic green bag hanging beside each leg.

"Hey, you get out of here."

Freeze steps away from Barry then turns toward the man. Lorilee wipes the tears from her good cheek and starts to stand up when she sees the man's eyes lower to the blade. Freeze goes into his stance, his left arm stretched out, his right hand raising the knife in front of him.

"You got a problem? Chink *fuck?*"

Lorilee sees the man's face stay as flat and as unmoving as in a picture. She looks at Barry slowly bending over to pick up the brown paper bag from the liquor store.

"Huh?" Freeze steps forward over the grease-soaked ground. "You fuckin' deaf? Motherfucker no speak English?"

Lorilee is shivering. She crosses her arms then holds back a scream that wants to come. She sees a fly land on the man's forehead just before his face changes and he drops both bags, jerks open the screen door, and runs back into the kitchen.

"*Book it,*" Barry says, hurrying past Freeze; then Lorilee is running too. Hearing Freeze behind her, she bends low under a metal box built into one of the brick walls then turns on the sidewalk where Barry did. She ignores the alternate lift and jarring pull of one breast then the other and runs wide-hipped and heavy through the clean cotton smell of tanned people after his bald head and moving blue-jeaned back, after Barry Raymond, who Glennie used to call a moron shitbag.

THE SUN HANGS FIERY in the haze above Sausalito Hills and Dave remembers studying maps every night of his first week west, sees himself sitting on the floor under the eye-numbing glare of his fluorescent light. Using his weight bench as a desk, he drew diagrams of all the major parallel streets then tested himself by sketching in the ones that intersected them and at what point. By the end of the week he felt ready enough to walk off San Pablo Street into the tiny fake marble-floored office of City Cabs, to lease a taxi from the huge woman behind the counter, a dirty red Peterbilt cap on her head, the name Ernestine printed on a black nameplate in front of her.

After his second night working the city he drove down Market Street looking for a place to park his cab and get a beer. He had just passed the darkened lobbies of tall office buildings, had looked through the ground-floor windows of some and seen the red-and-green light from security lamps reflecting off their shiny marble floors. Then he got to the plaza with the statue of the sailor in the middle. Before turning left onto Seventh he glanced over and saw them for the first time: all the men and women who live there at night. Under the hazy lime of the streetlights they lay curled up on the benches around the base of the green bronze statue, where, during the day, he had seen office workers sit to eat their lunches and read their papers. But then, his hands on the wheel, oblivious to the flash and tick of his indicator, all he saw were faces, some caked with drool and blood-vomit, the men's heavy-whiskered, the women's sagging, a few with soft fuzzy-looking beards under their chins. Another cabbie honked behind him, so Dave took the turn to the corner of Seventh and Market then locked his cab and walked into the neon light of the sidewalk past the open doors of bars breathing out electric beats heavy with bass. And just before stepping into the piss-wood cigarette smell of The Cat House Lounge, he looked over his shoulder at the plaza, a shiver skipping down his back.

Then he was walking out of the jukebox dark of it into a cold rain. The taste of peanuts and draft beer on his tongue, his hands in his pockets, he rocked back slightly on his heels, then caught himself when a man dressed in tight jeans and a bright red athletic club T-shirt stopped in front of him.

"God it's cold and wet, isn't it?"

But Dave was looking across the street to the rain-mist under the streetlights of the plaza, turned to the man as cool as if he had just been interrupted in conversation and said, "Yep." Then he crossed the slick asphalt of Market Street alone, and when he got to the sidewalk was already shaking his head. The rain was coming down slowly, but the droplets landed cold and heavy on his forehead and nose. He saw close to thirty of them lying on the benches, each in a cardboard box, their heads sticking out one end, their legs out the other. He stood and watched them, his shoulders hunched in his jacket.

Dave looks over his shoulder and backs out of the space, then drives straight ahead and turns left off Citadel Drive down the hill toward Berkeley. In the last gold light of day he passes neatly fenced-off gardens and trimmed lawns in front of wood and brick houses. He stops at the bottom of the hill then turns right onto Telegraph into the thick of the afternoon traffic. He looks to either side of him at students and well-dressed working people and a few of those scraggly-haired bearded creatures in torn clothes he knows someday he will be able to help, but not right now, not tonight. And he turns on the radio that is only AM but gets Springsteen rapping out a Jerry Lee Lewis beat. He begins to tap the wheel in time, moving his head to the screaming saxophone, smiling out his rolled-down window at two of those brown-eyed beauties walking on the sidewalk who he knows have probably lived in the States their whole lives and are as American as he, but still he can't stop seeing them on a torchlit veranda in white dresses, their black hair pulled to one side of their faces, the sky dark with stars over a mesquite desert; he would dance with them all night long over creaking boards, would kiss, then lick the taste of lime and salt out of their mouths. "I'm going to find one of *you*," he says loud enough for the two women to hear; they turn their heads to him and he puckers his lips for a kiss.

The red taillights of the cars ahead of him look brighter now. He drives past the cafés and bookstores of Berkeley, and he sees in them the comforting light that those places always seem to have. He looks to his left down San Jacinto, the sun completely gone now behind the dark stretch of hills across the bay, the sky filled with long thin clouds that hang crimson against the tangerine Pacific air. Tomorrow he would write that letter before he did anything else and if his father didn't like it then too goddamned bad because he wasn't paying for it anyway. Then he is looking straight ahead again, reaching to change radio stations, when he sees to his right just before the dark arch of the brick tunnel that takes San Pablo Street under a hill into El Cerrito, three people, one of them dark and slim, wearing sunglasses and a sleeveless denim jacket, his thumb out in the air.

WHEN THE BIG yellow taxi pulls over with a screech in front of Freeze, Lorilee turns her face away from Barry's warm open mouth and says, "But we don't have any money."

Barry looks at her with half-closed eyes. "Don't worry about it, Waters." Then he pulls her after him and Freeze, who has just opened the front door at the passenger side and climbed in. A hot wave rolling through her stomach, Lorilee follows Barry into the backseat then pulls the door shut beside her.

"El Cerrito, right?"

"Yeah," Freeze says.

Dave guides the old taxi back into the lighted stream of traffic and into the tunnel.

"You Berkeley students?"

"No," Freeze says.

"Just hanging out and taking it easy, huh?"

"Yeah."

Dave feels the silence before it comes; he reaches down to turn up the radio.

Freeze is tapping the armrest with his knuckles, trying to keep the rest of his body still. Lorilee sees him look at the thick sheath muscle in the driver's upper arm, its slight roll when he turns the knob on the radio, and as she watches, Freeze glances too at the swell of chest muscles that push tight against his T-shirt. They come out of the tunnel into the twilight and start down the hill.

"Where in El Cerrito, buddy?" Dave asks, smelling the booze now, the combination of that and young people and silence beginning to feel wrong to him; he reaches up to scratch a nonexistent itch at his temple then flexes his arm before bringing it back to the wheel.

"Don't matter." Freeze turns around to Barry and Lorilee sitting in the growing dark in the backseat, Barry's face looking oatmeal-colored, moonlike. Freeze lets his left arm drop behind the seat to touch Barry's knee. Lorilee looks at the hand, sees it tap Barry's leg then turn over fast and open-palmed. She watches it do the same movement again, this time faster. Then Barry's bulk shifts beside her as he moves to reach into his back pocket. She watches his pale closed fist move slowly to cover Freeze's hand. Freeze clears his throat loud as his thumb and forefinger flick open the blade of the black wood-handled knife. Dave looks over at the lean sunglassioed face to his right. "I can take you as far as Ernie's Pizza on San Pablo Street."

Freeze nods his head and Dave looks back at the road lit yellow now from the streetlamps. He looks in the rearview mirror at the pudgy one with the shaved head, at the blond girl with the most hound-doggish face he has ever seen, then he sees the huge bruise on her cheek and as quickly as Jell-O sliding off a plate, he feels the elation of just a few moments ago leave him.

Barry puts his arm around Lorilee but she doesn't let him pull her to him. She is looking at how tight Freeze seems to be gripping the knife, the blade pointing straight at the door behind the driver. She looks at the back of the driver's head then sees the clean-looking boylike face in the rearview. He's nice, she thinks. Then the driver's eyes move up to the mirror and are looking into hers. Lorilee looks away so fast she is afraid she might have made a noise. She looks at the side of Freeze's face, at his black oily hair, and she sees his eyes looking at the driver from behind his dark sunglasses, hears the tap of his knuckles above the radio, and she begins to rock back and forth on the seat, looks down again at the blade that shines every time they pass under a streetlight. She breathes fast and shallow as they uncoil dark and slick inside her, the pain of her buttocks having melted into something else now. And as Barry burps then drops his hand to her breast, she smells the stomach stench of his rum and closes her eyes to her nipple hardening under her shirt, to the moon-fixed feeling that this is it, this is what she has finally brought everyone to.

She feels the nervous squeeze of Barry's hand, and hears the static whine of radio music, the tappity tap tap of Freeze's knuckles in the front, the click of the lighted box that is showing how much they already owe. Then she hears sharp and clear the voice she has not let herself hear in months. *You're my ugly duckling girl, aren't you?* She opens her eyes.

Freeze's arm is pressed closer to the top of the seat, the knife just out of the driver's view, and Barry is squeezing harder and faster. Her heart is speeding and she hears her father again. She closes her eyes to the pinch-throb of Barry's fingers and gives in to it, is back in that hot bright kitchen, the fan broken and her father still dirty from the plant, his face sunburned and red from drinking too. *You're my ugly duckling girl, aren't you?* She looked at his mud-caked boots when he crossed the floor to her, and when he stood in front of her and unbuttoned her blouse she lifted her chin to his wide flat face.

Aren't you?

Yes, Papa.

Then he carried her into the room and laid her on the warm sheets. In the dark he undressed all of her. *My little ugly duckling, my little one.* Then he was inside her and it felt like tearing a scab and when the burn was gone it ached and she started to cry. He moved faster and then stopped and lay next to her and held her, and she pushed herself back against his hairy warm stomach, feeling so wrong.

Lorilee opens her eyes then pulls away from Barry's crazy hand, hears the driver's voice ask, "Are you all right, miss? Is he bothering you?"

Freeze says quietly, "She's all right."

"I'm not asking you, pal," Dave says into the dark sunglasses.

Barry's hand stops squeezing but still holds the flesh tight. "We're getting married, man," he says. "What's the problem?"

"What happened to your face, miss?"

"What's it to you?" Freeze asks.

Dave snaps his face to Freeze. "That's it. Ride's over for you, buddy."

"I ain't your buddy."

Dave pulls fast to the curb under the stringed and hanging lights of Arnold's Auto Sales. He points to the meter. "Four-sixty, smart ass." He picks up the notebook beside him. His hand is shaking. He lays it back on the seat then looks in the rearview to the big one looking back at him, a thin clear drool sticking to his chin. Dave looks at Lorilee rocking back and forth on the seat. "You don't have to go with them, miss."

"You hear me? I ain't your buddy."

Dave turns to Freeze. "Pay up and get out."

"We don't have no money," Barry says.

Dave looks away from Freeze to the mirror, to this smiling Frankenstein creature with his arm around this scared-to-death girl; his fleshy hand holding her breast. His heart beating in his throat, Dave turns around to look at Lorilee. "You don't have to go with these guys."

She is rocking, looking into the clean face of this driver. She sees the muscles in Freeze's forearm dance for an instant as the blade tilts up slightly. "Yes, Papa."

Barry jolts into laughter beside her, and then Freeze too; and Lorilee thinks, *Now,* you guys. *Now.* And she feels the cumulative weight and deed of her life rising up in her like a roller-coaster car nearing the peak of the highest and final run, the wind blowing different way up there, pushing quiet and steady against the side of her face. She rocks faster as the driver turns away from her and Barry to face Freeze who is smiling behind his sunglasses, who is raising the blade almost into view.

"Just get you and your freaky friends the hell out of—" Dave grunts as his head is jerked back against the headrest. He sees the stretched gray of ceiling above him and digs his fingers into the fat ones around his chin and mouth. "You fuck—"

Lorilee stops rocking; everything is moving fast now, and a laugh begins to well up from deep in her gut as Dave gets one hand free, then reaches back to grab a warm bristly head. Then his eyes are slapped over and covered by the hand of the dark quiet one. He begins to twist his torso and pull forward, hissing in air between the fingers that pull him; he sees himself pushing a barbell off his chest and tries to bring that same guttural cry out now as he yanks forward again.

"Suck this, faggot."

The hand of the dark one presses over his eyes then Dave feels the deep burn and rip of his insides; nausea shimmers through him then beads out clammy on his skin. He jerks away from the hard thing that slides out of him now and opens his eyes as the hand leaves too but his vision is hazy and he tastes the old metal of his blood rising in his throat. He opens and closes his mouth, trying to pump it out faster to breathe; he starts to spit as the liquid of him gushes warm down over the gripping hand of the big one. He is no longer able to pull now but just hold on, and he hears her high nasal laughter behind him, feels the buckle of his belt being pulled loose by the dark one, his coin box ripped free from his waist. He hears her laughing and feels the terrifying stop of everything as a groan comes up from his chest then ends in his throat. He breathes in deeply through his nose but his chest stays flat as he feels and hears his breath flap wetly out his side. Then the hands are gone and the car shifts as the doors open and he hears the dark one: "Leave the bitch. C'mon."

He hears the asphalt-patter of their running, his heart fluttering briefly in his chest that feels strapped now to the seat, then he opens his eyes to her horrible sound. From behind the mist of his nausea he sees her bending over, holding her stomach, her breasts hanging heavy. Her mouth wavers open but silent, she is laughing so hard. He pushes his loose-clenched fist into the heat of his side as Lorilee straightens, gets her breath, then shrieks and cackles tears down her bruised cheek. His chest beginning to lighten, the top of his head seeming to dissolve now into the air of his cab, Dave looks at the hanging stringed lights above her, watches how prettily the salt-shine of Lorilee's cheek catches the white glow of them. The pulse of him rises from his legs then passes quietly but quickly into his chest and he no longer hears the falsetto-wail of her laughing, so gives all of himself to what he can still see: her tear-filled blue eyes, and the long stringy blond hair that hangs in front of her reddened face. As his weight pulls itself in then up, through the hollow of his neck and to the top of his head, he looks back at the laughing girl, at the plum-purple bruise on her cheek, blue-black around the edges.

WOLVES IN THE MARSH

For Ande

When Dean awoke, the room was still cast in shadows and he smelled pee. He looked over at Kip's bed and saw him curled up with his knees almost touching his chin, his blanket sticking wet to the side of his leg. He was a year younger than Dean, eight, and he still wet his sheets at night, but so did Dean.

In the bathroom Dean peed but did not flush the toilet. He put the lid down then stood on it, and looked out the window through the bare tops of birch and beech trees to the sky. It was still a deep blue over the house and the slope leading down to the water, but it paled over the middle part of the lake and became a thin pink line just above the trees of the Boy Scout camp on the other side. The water was dark brown, almost black, and from the window the sand beach looked to Dean as white as bone.

He went back into his room and pulled on a pair of corduroy pants, a T-shirt, and Kip's blue sweater. He found some socks that didn't match but were thick, and so pulled them on and laced his boondocker boots on over them. He took his BB rifle from the corner, laid it on his bed, then pulled a sock full of BBs out of the top right drawer of his bureau and tied the hanging bulge to his front belt loop. He picked up his rifle and looked down at sleeping Kip and his pee spot; he thought about waking him up but then saw himself walking through the woods alone with his gun and huge supply of ammunition, not having to take turns to shoot or anything. He pressed the sockful of BBs against his thigh, went quickly down the stairs and out the door.

The porch was open on all sides and overlooked the water through the trees. Dean stepped off it and made his way down the slope, over exposed pine roots, to the gravel road in front of the lake. He stopped there and looked out over the water at the thin trails of mist that hovered and glided on its surface. Something splashed beside the tall water reeds near the beach and Dean looked and saw the flick of a fin before it went under. He started down the road away from the water and the house into the woods. He saw his breath in front of him as he walked by the summer cottages that were built close to the lake, and when he was past them, he could see the wide bend of the river through the trees. It began on the other side of his house where the lake made a small cove then flowed under a short wooden bridge to the marsh. It widened there then pushed itself all the way to the Atlantic Ocean, about twenty miles to the northeast, his father had told him; his father told him and Kip lots of things, like how moss grows on the north side of trees and it's better to take a dirty skillet and wash it down on the beach with sand because soap isn't good for the black iron. His father had been in the marines, a captain, and sometimes before they ate, he would have Jody and Dean and Kip and Simone hold their hands out for inspection, see if they were clean enough.

Dean walked along the road holding his rifle in front of him with two hands and letting the sockful of BBs bounce and sway against his leg. He was past all the summer houses now and into a part of the woods that was so thick with evergreen trees it was almost always dark here; even in the summer, during the hottest and brightest time of the day, when the mosquitoes would sting everywhere, even through Dean's clothes, this place would be shadows where only scattered rays of light made it all the way to the ground. But this morning, with the sun still barely on the other side of the lake, the woods appeared so dark to Dean he felt he was almost in a cave. And there was frost everywhere; he saw the thin icy layer of it on the moss patches at the base of the trees, and the brown pine needles that blanketed the floor of the woods were covered with it. He stopped walking and sat beside the road. He rested his rifle on his thighs, unscrewed the long thin tube beneath the barrel, then untied the sock at his belt loop. He reached into it for a handful of BBs and dropped them one at a time into the tube's tiny hole until his hand was almost empty and he no longer heard the BBs roll down to meet the others but stop just inside the magazine. He screwed the tube back into place, tied his sock to his side, then stood and slapped the cold pine needles from the seat of his pants. The woods were very quiet and he heard only the skitter of what he thought might be a chipmunk or a squirrel, then dead pine twigs falling to the ground, but no birds. Dean knew from his fourth-grade teacher, Miss Williams, that a lot of New Hampshire birds fly south for the winter; but it wasn't winter yet, just November, and even if the others had left already, the woodpecker and whippoorwill were supposed to stay behind to hibernate in thick nests and tree holes.

Dean walked farther down the road to where it split off and went in two directions. He stayed on the right fork, which he knew would take him deeper into the woods to where he could no longer hear the big eighteen-wheelers that he began to hear now. The left fork led to those; and Dean started to walk faster; but it wasn't that he did not like highways and cars and trucks—they were okay—though he found he could not get as excited about them as his friend Clayton and the other boys in school. During quiet time before lunch, they drew pictures of dragsters and dune buggies while Dean read books about Kit Carson, Daniel Boone, and Wild Bill Hickock. And after school, when he would walk one or two or three miles into the woods, it was not to hear the whiz and whoosh of cars and trucks; when he was deep into them, down on the river side in the spring and fall when the mosquitoes were not so bad, when he would come to a place between two trees where the ground was so thick with fallen pine needles that he felt he could almost bounce on it, and so would lie down on it, and look up at the sky past the tips of evergreen trees that must have taken root sometime around the Civil War, Dean felt that there was nowhere else he ever wanted to be. He would hear a bobwhite call out from somewhere near the river. He would close his eyes then catch the dirt scent of the decayed pine needles beneath him. And with his eyes shut, he would feel the bigness of things around him, but it was a big with soft places and nice smells and familiar sounds, and so he never felt afraid there.

Dean kept walking but did not know how far down the right fork he would go, maybe just as far as that place with all the hemlock trees. The last time he had been there it was a week before last Christmas and he and his father and Kip, and even Simone, had walked to it the day after a blizzard to cut down a Christmas tree. His father had worn his machete at his side and Dean had liked the look of it slapping against his leg as they made their way through the snow. Then Kip found a good tree, and they had watched as their father had cut it down and pulled it out onto the road. The woods had gotten very dark then, and Simone said that her toes were frozen, but she had begged to come and their father had to drag the tree, so he told her she was just going to have to march it out with the rest of the troops. She did, Dean remembered, but she had cried a little bit, too.

Dean cocked his gun, aimed at the thin white trunk of a birch tree, and squeezed the trigger. He felt the recoil of the spring with his finger and heard the tick of the BB against the wood. He cocked his rifle again then looked for something else to shoot, wishing a bird or a squirrel would show up. Or maybe even a bigger animal. No, not a bigger animal, he thought, and he walked off the road in the direction of the river and sat down, resting his back against the scarred trunk of a tall beech tree. He was aware of his fingers and the tip of his nose, and he wished he had taken Jody's gloves from her coat pockets. But then he thought how he wouldn't be able to load and shoot with them on his hands. He rested his rifle on his outstretched legs and tried to ignore the rumble of his stomach, and he remembered that Kit Carson book he read this past summer, the parts about the fur trapping and how Kit would go days sometimes eating only snow and sucking the bark of certain kinds of trees. Dean thought about that: sitting in the snow sucking bark for breakfast. And he thought of that morning last winter when he had gone into the kitchen for another bowl of cereal and had seen his mother and father sitting at the table. His mother was leaning forward and was talking in a quick low voice, and his father was listening, smoking a cigarette, and his face had looked calm, almost peaceful, like it did whenever Dean would see him listen to one of his jazz records for the first time—relaxed, but trying to feel what it was he was supposed to feel—and it didn't seem to Dean to be the right face to have on because his mother's was all tight while she spoke. When he saw that, Dean had stopped where he was in the doorway and heard her say, "You goddamned ma*rine*." And he had not known why she had said it like that, because he liked that part about his father. He liked the way his voice could fill up the rooms of the house like his mother's couldn't, even when she was mad.

Dean pulled the trigger and heard the BB dance its way through the branches above him. He stood to cock his rifle, and when he did, he heard the hollow tapping sound of a woodpecker working up ahead of him and to his left. He knew how noises could fool you in the woods, though, especially when there was water nearby, and as he walked forward in a crouch, stepping lightly over sticks and twigs that broke dry under his feet, he looked up at the middle third of the trees and scanned them from east to west. He heard it again, but this time it seemed to be coming from his right. He walked straight ahead until he came to a swell in the ground that dropped steeply to the marsh. He paused there and looked out over it and the river, which he had never tried walking to before because in the spring the marsh was covered with water, and now in fall, almost winter, it looked like it could swallow you; there were clumps of earth covered with grass the color of straw, and in between them were dark ribbons of mud that looked to Dean like they would open up under his feet and suck him under.

But in the summer the water grass would be green and yellow and three or four feet tall and when a breeze blew through them, Dean would watch them all bend in dry rolling waves like they were bowing down to the powers of the earth. But now, early in the morning and just before winter, when the straw clumps lay matted and weighted down with frost, Dean thought that the marsh looked as dangerous as ever—a flat wet land a man would have to face to get to the water for pickerel and bass. There was mist on the river, but Dean could still see its quiet swirling surface. Above the trees the sky was bathed in a pale gray light, and Dean wondered what had happened to the sun he had seen the beginnings of on the other side of the lake.

The air was cold and a little damp, and it felt as if it might even snow. He thought of winter coming, how it's the only season that stays like it will never leave; and he thought of last winter and how everything first started then; he remembered how he and Kip and Jody and Simone used to all sit together at the top of the stairs to listen and sometimes giggle until their mother would come yell up at them to quit being so nosy and to go to bed. Her face had looked okay then, almost cheerful, but then spring came, and summer, and that's when all the parties started, that's when almost every weekend people from his father's college would come over and there would always be lots of music and loud talk and laughing, and sometimes crying, too. And on those hot late nights after everyone had gone home, Dean could hear his mother and father over the whir and rattle of the window fan. He would go out to the lighted hallway to listen and once he saw his older sister Jody sitting on the top stair in her nightgown. He sat down beside her, and they listened together. They sat there for a long time, and it had felt to Dean that what they were doing was very important, that if he and Jody could only figure out why their mother and father were fighting, then they could go tell Kip and Simone and, together, the four of them could all help to fix it. Then he had heard their mother interrupt their father and say, "Oh shut up! Just shut up!" And Dean had felt afraid, but Jody had burst out laughing and so he did too, and when their mother came to the bottom of the stairs her face had not looked cheerful but tired, very tired, and then angry as she told them, "This is none of your business, now go to bed right this goddamned *min*ute." And Dean had gone to bed, but later, lying in the dark with his sheet pulled up to his chin, he had felt that something big and dangerous was going on downstairs and that if he ignored it and went to sleep, he would wake up in a house on fire.

Dean aimed his rifle over the marsh at the river. He pulled the trigger but did not see the tiny splash of a BB. Probably sucked down into the marsh, he thought. He cocked his rifle again then just stood there with it. He liked this picture of himself standing on a hill with his loaded gun, guarding the woods and his family from whatever might try to crawl out of the marsh to get them. And he thought of wolves swimming across the river then making their way through the straw clumps and mud with their tongues hanging out and their fangs all foamy. He would lie down on his belly and pick them off one at a time, but with a BB gun it would be harder because he would have to hit them in the eyes to blind them and he would do it too, aiming, taking his time, then shooting the way his father had shown him, not pulling the trigger but squeezing it, hitting each wolf once in each eye until the whole pack of them would just stop in the marsh to grope and stumble through the mud, bleeding and howling at the darkness.

Dean listened for the woodpecker but only heard the faint but constant scurrying of what sounded to him like hundreds of ants and termites and spiders and ladybugs and crickets as they finished their morning feeding and went about their day getting ready for winter. And at the thought of food, Dean turned away from the marsh to head back for the road. But then he saw it: to his left and down the slope, almost in the marsh, was a tall dead pine tree. It was stripped of its bark in some places; its branches were thick broken stumps; and the top third of it lay on the ground at its base. The woodpecker was perched at the very top of the broken tree, darting its beak in and out of the hole it had made while its thin legs clutched at the bark. It was the yellow-tailed kind Dean saw mainly in the summer and he raised his BB rifle and put the bird in his sights, but he knew it was too high and out of range, so he lowered his gun and began to walk down the slope. He kept his eyes on the bird as he made his way down the incline, but some of the pine needles were giving way under his boots so he looked in front of him every few steps as he went. When he reached flat ground he felt it turn soggy and he could smell the wet grass from the marsh. It's a very bad smell, he thought, like crap almost. He heard the woodpecker again, but it had stopped the hard drilling part of its work and was sticking its beak into the hole then pulling it out again, letting tiny chips of wood drop all the way to the ground so close to Dean that he could not believe it did not know he was there. He spread his legs and planted his boots in the soft ground. Then he raised his rifle and put the yellow strip of the bird's wing feathers in his sights. I'll hit it there, he thought, right there, and he held his breath and squeezed the trigger. At first it felt like a BB hadn't left the barrel at all, but just a little blast of air. It did that sometimes, misfired like a real gun, and he lowered it quickly to cock it again, but when he did, he saw two single yellow feathers floating down the length of the tree. He looked up at the woodpecker and saw it pull its beak out of the hole; then it raised its wings and released itself from the tree, but instead of flying forward it flew backward, out over the marsh, treading air with quick awkward flaps of its wings. The bird's beak was still facing the tree, and it seemed to Dean that it was looking straight into the hole, trying to understand how this had come to happen. Then Dean saw a feather come away, then another; the woodpecker flapped its wings in a flurry, stopped, then flapped them once more before it went still, and dropped straight into the marsh.

For what seemed to him a very long time, Dean stood with his boots sunk firmly in the ground. His rifle hung down by his side and he held it with one hand. He was looking at the spot where the bird had landed; it was a straw thicket surrounded by a ring of mud and it reminded Dean of the castles and moats in the King Arthur books Miss Williams sometimes read out loud before lunch. But he could not see the bird, and he hoped that it was lying in the straw and hadn't bounced behind the thicket into the bad-smelling mud. He wanted to go get it and make sure it was dead, but he knew he would not step into the marsh to try. He felt his face flush as he thought of Kit Carson; he knew if Kit had just killed an animal, even a skinny woodpecker, he would not let it go to waste but would eat it, or at least use the feathers for something, like to make an earmuff or a necklace. And he wished his father were out here in the woods with him; then he could watch him walk out into the marsh in his marine boots to get the bird, and if it was still alive, well then they could shoot it real fast in the head to put it out of its misery. Maybe his father could show him how to skin it too. Dean had never heard of anyone eating a woodpecker before, but he knew people ate other little birds, like doves. He looked out at the marsh and the quiet river and the trees beyond it. He felt the woods at his back and he could not remember them ever seeming so quiet. He stepped toward the marsh but his boot sunk in up to his laces and he pulled it out, and stepped back.

By the time Dean reached the fork in the road it had already begun to snow. It was an icy snow, and it made a thousand little ticking noises through the trees as it fell, but Dean only saw a few flakes and they were the ones that came down through the space between the treetops over the road. The air felt colder to him and he was very hungry. He wondered if anyone was up yet. It was Saturday, a cartoon day, and he imagined Jody and Simone sitting on the floor in front of the TV with bowls of Captain Crunch in their laps. When he came to the summer cottages he could see the woods opening up ahead of him. His rifle was not cocked and when he walked by the last cottage before he came to the lake and the slope leading up to his house, he did not turn to put another tiny hole in the bathroom window that he sometimes shot at for target practice. I don't need it anymore, he thought as he came out onto the road below his house. He looked up at it and it seemed to him that sleeping was still going on inside of it. Snowflakes landed lightly but wet on his face and he saw that they were beginning to make the hill white, but he knew that it was not cold enough yet and they would not cover the ground for long. He looked out at the lake and saw that the mist had gotten thicker. He could barely see the water and the sky was gray and looked huge and heavy, like it had just come closer to the earth to drop its snow. The dock was white now, too, and Dean turned and began to walk down the road toward the wooden bridge between the lake and the river.

The gravel felt hard beneath his boots, but it was dusted white, and he remembered how thick with frost the driveway behind the house was as they all followed their father out to the car, two Sundays ago. Kip and Simone were still in their pajamas and had put their boots and coats on over them, but Dean and Jody were all dressed and Jody even wore her gloves. When they got to the car, Dean had looked into it and seen it packed full of clothes and boxes of books, and he pictured his father staying up all night, loading it while they slept. Their mother had stayed in the kitchen and Dean wished she had come outside, too. Then they heard her crying turn into a long, high wail; and it had sounded to Dean like the noise a deer might make. His father opened the car door and turned to face the four of them. He was smiling but there were tears on his cheeks and in his moustache. He bent down and picked up Simone first, and Dean watched him shut his eyes tight as he hugged her. When he put her down Jody moved to him quickly and kissed him on the mouth before she put her arms around his neck. Their mother's crying was getting louder in the house and Dean watched his father try to smile again with his wet face as he pulled away from Jody, turned to him and Kip, and then hugged them both together. Dean's shoulder had hurt pushing against Kip's, but when he smelled his father's aftershave lotion, he had kissed him on the neck.

"I'll be seeing y'all in just a few days," his father had said. "And this weekend we'll see a movie and go out to eat. Okay?"

They were all quiet as he got into his old car and started it, then backed up, and headed down the hill. Dean watched it move slowly toward the bridge, the exhaust from its tailpipe turning blue in the cold air. He was no longer aware of his brother and sisters standing beside him, or his mother crying in the house; he could see the back of his father's head through the rear window and he wished he had said something strong or funny for him, so that he would not worry about them out here in the woods alone. Then Kip had scooped up a handful of gravel and run down the hill and threw it, but their father's car had already reached the bridge, and Dean only hoped that he had had his window rolled up and was not looking in the rearview mirror.

Dean looked out at the lake. It was the same color as the sky, and he knew it was cold, but with the mist covering it, it looked to him like one big hot bath. He turned away from it and walked over to the other side of the bridge. He saw mist there too, thin white flumes of it skimming along the moving surface of the river. He knew the snow was doing this, but it looked to him like the mist was coming from the marsh. He rested his rifle against the railing, then leaned forward to try to see where the river cut to the west before it made its curve northeast. But all he saw were the evergreen trees at the base of the hill behind his house, and then the marsh, more sunk in white than the river even.

He picked up his rifle and walked off the bridge and started the climb up the gravel driveway to the rear of his house. He was so hungry now that his stomach didn't rumble anymore and he wanted only orange juice. When he reached the top of the hill there was already enough snow on the driveway so that he could barely see the pebbles of the gravel beneath it. He climbed the back stairs and the sockful of BBs rolled on and off his thigh. He heard TV noises coming from inside the house, and he wondered if his brother and sisters knew it was snowing outside. Cool flakes melted wet on his face, and as he opened the back door of the porch and leaned his rifle against the wall, he imagined the snow as it fell into the marsh; the mist would lift as the air got colder and the straw and mud became a blanket of white. The snow would stay all winter and in the spring Dean would walk into the woods, maybe even with Kip; they would follow the right fork until just before the hemlocks. Then they would walk off the gravel road toward the marsh. They would come to a little hill where they would stop and look out over the wide and swollen river. It would be all the way to the base of the slope, covering everything, even the bottom three or four feet of the pine tree. Dean would be holding his rifle and Kip would be carrying the BBs, and together they would just stand there, he and his brother, watching the high water as it flowed over the marsh, and carried all the dead things to the sea.

FORKY

My coffee's gone cold and I look at her over the rim of my cup. I look at her throat, at the tiny part that moves as she talks. I listen to her life and I know when to nod my head and when to smile. But my stomach tightens as I try and look like I know what she's saying. I see her naked, her belly against mine. And I think how she was probably still intact my first year down.

Johnny looked too much like my brother Marty with his smooth face and small shoulders, and when I saw him that first time at the commissary, I knew I wouldn't let this kid fall, not this one. And I'd been in for four, three more to go. And nobody fucked with me after the first two. They called me Forky.

I was a first offender. And I never would've gone down if I had listened to Marty, if I hadn't a used the .38. But I did. And when that fat manager went for me I turned and stuck it in his face, watched him turn to butter. And before I knew it I'd gone from County to the state pen at Canon. Five to ten for armed robbery. And I couldn't even cry.

That was the last time I saw Marty. An hour or so at County before Canon. He said to get a rep right away, to watch for the lifers. Then he said the words and I said them back. And I was glad I said them. And I thanked Jesus I said them after that letter came from my sister in Jersey, three years down the road.

I light her cigarette and watch my hand shake. And I know it's not the coffee 'cause I drink a shitload of it. I'm wondering why she's taking all this time with me, and I think it can't be the free drinks. She don't seem the type. And even though she ain't one of the most beautiful women I've ever seen, she's all right. And I want to tell her where I've been. But I wait.

It was my sixth day in the joint. And the word was out that I was Leroy and Wallace's lady-in-waiting. Wallace was the biggest. At mess I looked and found his bald brown head, shining like the corridors after lights out and looking just as hard. He was at the end of the table near the aisle, and looking back now, there wasn't nothing to it at all.

They don't let you eat with metal. So I had to settle for plastic. And I knew I'd have to get a running start to do the damage I wanted to do. So three tables before his I lengthened my stride, picked up speed. And my heart was beating so fast I didn't think I'd be able to line it up right. But then Wallace looked up and his black eyes caught me and he flashed that gold-toothed smile, the one that says, "You's mine." And that's all I needed. I drove it in fast and twisted quick so that my fork broke off inside. Then Wallace was up with a kind of grunt-hiss, then a wail as he fell over backwards off the bench. He wouldn't let go of my arm and it was warm and wet with that shit from his eye. I wanted to wipe it off, but then there were the guards and it was lights out.

She asks me why I don't talk much and I tell her I like to listen. Then I tell her she's beautiful and she gives me that look I ain't seen in seven and a half years. The one that says I don't believe you, but thanks anyway. I ask her to dance. It's a slow one and I can't believe I'm smelling a woman, this close. And I remember junior high. Me and Be Bop Little. She had the biggest ones in school and all the guys used to call her Be Bop Floppity Flop. Once I got her for a slow dance and I had to pull away I got so hard. I have to pull away from this one, too. Just a little. She looks up and gives me a half smile with her lips. And I swallow hard.

Johnny was a smart one. Even though I was older and bigger, sometimes he'd make me feel young and small around him. He was always reading a book. Always writing to the warden and his PO. Always talking a couple of dudes out of a fight and the hole. And he always had a string a top-notch jokes when we were drinking at night. I remember him after his first shot of tomato jack. Man, he hugged me like a sonuvabitch. Couldn't believe he wasn't gonna go five more years without a snort or two. Then he found out it was a secret formula. So he typed the recipe up one night and passed it out to all the joes in B.

The number's over and I'm so nervous I jump off the wagon and switch over to a CC on the rocks, a double. She's not talking as much, and I think how I don't want her to get stiff. I don't want my first time to be with someone who's not gonna remember. So I down my drink and ask her if she wants to go for a walk. I get her a pack a cigarettes at the machine by the door. Then we're outside.

It's almost cold, not too bad, just enough to wake you up and clear your head. The stars are out and you can smell the snow, because it's city snow.

"Where'd you get a name like Forky?" she says.

I stop and look down at her, like it's the first thing I've heard her say all night, and I think how young she looks for having two kids already. Then I take a deep drag off my cigarette and look straight ahead as we walk.

I did ninety days in the hole for gouging Wallace. And in all that time, in all that emptiness and quiet, I never stopped being scared. And then the voices made it worse. And when I got out I was so scared I must've been the meanest motherfucker in Old Max. And then I found out about Wallace, about him almost killing one of his own boys for using my name around him. And when I heard that I knew I'd taken something out of him. I knew he wouldn't come after me alone. So I got a shank.

We walk up the street and it's pretty quiet 'cause it's a Tuesday night. There's still some ice on the walk and I let her hold my arm so she don't slip. She smells nice and I feel myself start to swell again. I think I should start talking more so I start to ask her her kids' names. But when I do my voice sounds phony, like it's in a deep hole that it's gotta shout at to get out of, but it's gotten so used to the hole that it don't even try anymore. So I leave it alone. She's come this far without it.

A bus swings around us on the corner of Fifth and Euclid. I see people in it. They're all staring straight ahead and their faces look gray in that light, like wax. And for an instant I get a chill, deep, like a shock. I turn and pull her towards me. She's got surprise on her face. But it ain't hard; it's soft. So I lean into her and she tastes like gin, but she's warm and she lets me use my tongue as she slides hers over and under mine. I feel a sudden weakness, but I'm hard and I pull her closer. I want her to feel it, to know it. And when she doesn't stiffen up on me I feel like my soul is being offered back. And for a second I see Ma, washing my hands for me, hers bigger than mine, all slippery and warm with the soap and water. And it feels like medicine.

It was rec time and me and Johnny was in the yard. I had gotten him into my routine and we had just finished, red and sweating like bastards. I straightened up to walk and Johnny headed for the fountain in the shadows of the tier. I had just started when I froze still. I remembered Leroy's face my sixth or seventh time around the yard, he and one of the brothers under the tier. And running back towards it I knew something was going down 'cause it was quiet there, empty. And I knew they was in the blind, that corner no tower guard could see around.

By the time I got around it I had my shank out, and when that first sonuvabitch turned his head I sliced him clean right beneath the hairline. Then Leroy turned towards me and that's when I saw Johnny, a flash of him, white as a ghost, but breathing. Leroy got in a crouch.

"Uh, big man heah. Big man mothuh Fork. Watchoo want mothuh Fork?"

His shank was catching the light of the sun as he turned it over in his hand. But I wasn't even there, man. I was five stories up, calm and together, watching, waiting for my move. Waiting for the burn. And I didn't give a fuck. I wanted him. So I stopped and stood and let him come. And when he did I shifted to the side and let him come into it himself. I aimed high and caught him in the shoulder.

"Cocksuh!"

He moved again, this time wildly, and I got ahold of his knife hand then cut him again in the same place, jabbing hard till I struck bone. His arm went limp against mine and I butted him hard in the chin with my head. And down there in the dirt, breathing hard and holding his own wound, he didn't have no fear in his eyes. But I could smell it, man. And I could feel it too, cold and clammy. So could Johnny, 'cause that's when he came up from behind and gave him a good swift kick to the back of his head, snapping Leroy's big mouth to his chest before he went out. Then we were outta there. Running and laughing like whores, fucking giddy with ourselves, man. Scared shitless.

Her place is small and it smells like laundry and fruit. She pays the sitter, young and fat, chewing gum. Then we're alone. In the kitchen she pours us gin and in this light I see the crow's-feet at the corner of her eyes, the tiny hard look of her hands as she cuts the limes. I look at the walls, at all the kiddy drawings lining the room, and I see me and Marty slugging it out over a box of crayons. She hands me my drink and I think how much I like brown eyes, the way they take you deep down somewhere, and then it just comes out.

"I've spent the last seven years of my life in the joint." She don't say nothing. Just looks at me.

"Prison," I say. For an instant I see myself back on the street, breathing the cold, heading for the north side of town, back to my one-room where I gotta keep the shades down so the streetlight don't keep me up. Then her eyes take me deeper.

"I've spent that time working and raising two kids, mostly alone."

"Yeah, but I was in jail."

"And I was married." We laugh and I feel shaky again. She sees it. So we sit and drink our gin.

Johnny'd pulled all the boys together after mess and told 'em how short I was. A few of them came in one at a time during the night. Mac brought me a milk carton full of raisin jack. And he only stayed for a shot. He had eight more to go before parole, but he was warm, man.

"You motherfucker, Fork. Take care of yourself."

Valdez and Leary came in together. Valdez was like always, dark-eyed and quiet, but Leary was talking like a sonuvabitch.

"Man, it ain't gonna be the same, Forky. Who's gonna be the great white hope now, motherfucker? Who's gonna put it to 'em like you done?"

"Johnny's in trainin' for the spot, ain't ya John boy?"

"Damn straight," Johnny said. Then he took a deep one off the jack. He looked so little there then and I was sorry I said it. I offered them some jack, but they knew how tight me and Johnny was and they didn't want to work on our last bottle together.

"Well, what the hell, Fork." Leary gave me his hand. "Get some for me, man. Hot and juicy." On the way out Valdez handed me his crucifix and gave me sort of a bow, like he was Chinese or something.

Johnny passed me the carton and I had all my shit taken care of so I swallowed two or three times. Man, it was Mac's best, like brandy.

"You going back east, Forky?"

"I don't know, man. I been thinking about hanging out on the eastern slope awhile. I mean, shit, Johnny, you're a short timer, too. Almost as short as me. I was thinking about hanging around till you're processed out. Then you and me go back east and let 'em know what's fuckin' what. You and me Johnny."

I passed the jack back feeling for the first time a lot bigger and a little older, and it gave me a kind of shudder. That's when I handed him my shank. He had the carton held to his mouth and when he saw it he stopped. Then he looked straight ahead and drank.

"You use it, motherfucker."

He was smiling at me.

"If the man comes, put it in his fucking gut. No hesitation."

He was sitting there looking at me, looking small and wise again. And I knew that he'd keep it in his fuckin' house, that he wouldn't carry it.

"I ain't bullshittin', Johnny." He took another swig then passed it back to me.

"Hey, Fork." He reached over and started scratching my head. "What's this?"

"It's your fuckin' ass-wiping hand."

"Nope. It's a brain eater."

"Yeah, so?"

"What's it doing?"

"Beats me, Johnny boy." Then he looked me in the face, real serious, already a little glassy with the jack.

"Starving." Then he let loose, laughing like no tomorrow. He stretched out his legs and went into his high-pitched laugh.

I looked at his little body shaking on the mattress. Then I got it, but lifted the carton quick so he couldn't see me smile.

I look at myself in the mirror. Not bad. Still lean. I look at her deodorants and perfumes, her floss and skin cream, and I wonder how I got here. Then I find the pink razor and I use soap and hot water and shave as close as I can. But she uses it on her legs and I cut myself twice on the chin. And I feel the same way I did with Bertha back in Jersey eleven years ago. She was big and black and she'd been taking kids' cherries for years. The neighborhood man maker. Marty had it all fixed up, and I think I only spent two hours in the bathroom before. Shaving, zit cream, aftershave, mouthwash, deodorant, and I finally decided to keep my rubbers tucked in my skivvies for quick reference. I'm more than nervous, but there's something else. I check my face. There's something else. I wait until the blood stops, then I go to her room.

She's sitting up in bed, smoking, the sheet covering her, and I like how small her shoulders look. But I'm rubbery all over and I feel a sudden urge to just sit across the room and let somebody else do it.

"I thought people got fat in jail."

I suck in my gut then show her my arms. She laughs. I drop my skivs and slide in next to her. She reaches over to the bedstand and passes me a drink. I see she's already got one.

"I need this," I say.

"Seven years is a long time."

"Seven and a half. I feel like Rip van Winkle." I laugh.

"You don't look it." She's smiling. And I think how confident she looks knowing she's gonna be the one to give it to me. I down the rest and pass her back my glass.

I woke up dry and heavy-eyed from the jack. And I'd already pissed and washed before it hit me all at once; hit me in my stomach, my fingertips and toes, my hung-over head, that, man, I was never gonna wake up in this fuckin' place again! I was hyper as a sonuvabitch. Ripped the sheet and blanket off my bed. Rolled the mattress and put it against the wall. Folded the linen and put it on the springs. Then grabbed my shaving kit and bounced on my toes a few times before the cells opened. My escort guard was late so I decided to head down to processing myself.

D Block had been mine. And moving through it, I memorized the faces, the cells, the clean tile, and gray brick. Some of the guys slapped me on the back or punched me light in the arm.

"Do it, motherfucker."

"Taste it, Fork."

And when I got to the passage at C, I fought it and didn't turn around. I was walking pretty fast, breathing real easy, and I was halfway through C before I noticed. Nobody was around. Even slow Joe Fernandez was up and outta his cell. But there was more. Something else. And I did what I always did when I felt that way in the joint, I reached around and checked my shank. I felt my belt and my skin through my shirt. Then I remember and I'm running. The first part of B is empty, too. Then I see them, all crowded around, a bunch a blue-shirts, and I plow into them. Watch it, motherfucker! I'm pushing to the center and I feel the way I used to get with Marty jumping the bridge for the bay; you're free-falling and you want to hurry up and hit 'cause the weight of your whole body has moved up to your head, but at the same time you don't want to stop moving. Then I see his feet and I scream "No, motherfucker! No!" And she's outta bed and she's holding me and I swing away from her and slam my head into her wall and it ain't brick, the fucking wall ain't brick! Then I'm up and reeling. I'm in the cell and the first guard is still cutting Johnny's hands loose and I scream "No, motherfucker! No, motherfucker! No!" And his face is blue and gray, like candle wax, and his eyes are bulged out like a fucking fish, and I'm swinging and she's saying "Shut up! My kids!" And the guards're holding me and I pull away and wrap my arms around little Johnny and he smells the way he did when I hugged him in the hall, when I said the words and he fucking said them back! Like a boy! Then the other smell hits me and I know if the motherfuckers could write it'd be: To Forky, Best Wishes, Leroy and Wallace. And I want to die. And I want them dead. And I want them dead through me, and the guards're holding me and the Doc's putting it in my arm, and I scream "No!

No!" And she's dressed and she's pulling me, the door's shut and I reach for the curtain, but the water's beating down on me cold and I think how they must've done it right after lights out. He's so cold, so fucking cold.

"Johnny, you sonuvabitch. You're almost as short as me, you sonuvabitch. Johnny. You sonuvabitch."

She's with me. All wet. And she's got eye makeup on her cheeks. She ain't dressed anymore, and I just keep crying. I see the letter about Marty. I kept it for almost a year and I thought I'd cry, but I never did. And I feel the weight of the hole, ninety days and still not a tear. I was ten and it was hot out. You had to have shoes on in the street and you couldn't lean against the cars without a shirt. And I kept bringing the bucket back into the kitchen, filling it up, then back outside and I'd throw half on my friend and he'd dump half on me, then I did it again and again. And Ma was sick and she came out smelling funny and her hair was all messed up and her face was white and she slapped my face and said, "I hate you!" I ran outside and it came out of me like a flood.

MOUNTAINS

I lie next to him and feel his breathing, so shallow and light, and I pray he's not dreaming about that place again. Last night he woke me up. He had his hand on my shoulder, squeezing real hard, and he said, "Charlie's out there. This place is fuckin' crawling with Charlie." I touched his hand and he let go. Then I turned towards him and smelled his sweat.

"Everything's fine, babe. I'm here. Everything's fine," I said. I kissed his cheek and tasted the salt. Then he put his arms around me and curled up his legs, said into my breasts, "Fuck 'em."

I get up first, go to the bathroom and pee. I finish, then flush, and I know he'll wake up with just that little sound. I pull my hair back and hold it with one hand while I brush my teeth. Then I rinse out my mouth and avoid the mirror as I put the towel to my face.

I turn on the radio in the kitchen, keep it low because it's rock and because I want to hear him when he gets up. It was bad last night and I don't know if he's going to wake up numb, if he'll come into his day feeling nothing about everything, looking at me with the eyes you use on a stranger.

I break the eggs into the bowl of milk, beat them with a fork, then melt the butter and get the bread, dip two slices and lay them flat and sizzling into the skillet. I turn off the heat under the water and pour it into the pot, letting the coffee smell steam up into my face. I pour myself a cup, take it out to the porch.

Lumpy is curled up in her box next to Rick's gear, her little gray paw covering her face. Her bowl is still full, and I look through the screen at the mountains. They're always so blue just before the sun comes up, their peaks pointing white like shark's teeth against the sky. I remember the drive up from Pueblo last August. It was sunny and bright and we drove along the foothills all the way. When we went through Colorado Springs I kept my eyes on Pike's Peak, so tall and blocky-looking, and I didn't feel small looking at it, but big, because I was with Rick. And when I couldn't see it anymore I looked at him then wrapped my arms around his neck, kissed him on his ear and cheek. He turned his face a little to me, smiling, and I said, "This is going to be so good, Ricky!" Then we kissed until the wheels started bumping and he had to break away to steer.

I sip my coffee and smell leather and cat pee, Rex's feed. I turn and go back into the kitchen. He's pouring himself a cup, his back to me, and I look at his messed-up hair, his shirttail hanging out over his jeans. I move behind him and turn over the French toast.

"What time is it?"

"Close to six." I look into his face. He turns away, looks over the table and out the window. He sips from his coffee.

"Rick. I know it was bad last night." I go to him, put my hands on his chest, pull myself in close. "I love you, Ricky."

"It's getting worse." He turns and puts his cup on the counter, pushes me a little with his arm.

"Call Reuben again."

"I can't talk to that motherfucker, you know that."

I get him a plate, flip the bread slices out of the skillet, and set it on the table.

"Sit down. Eat."

He finishes the rest of his coffee and lights a cigarette. "I'm not hungry." He walks past me to the porch and I feel myself hold it in.

"Get out of here, cat!"

Lumpy comes around through the door, rubs up against my shin. I squat down and run my fingers over her ears. Then he's at the door, the tack and saddle over his shoulder, his hat in his hand. He looks at me like he's about to say something but then turns around quick and walks out the door and down the steps. I look down at Lumpy and my eyes fill up, then I watch him through the screen door on his way to the truck, see him look real quick from side to side, looking for them, waiting, and I try and remember some of his stories; I see the little girl out in the paddy, the morning mist covering her feet, all that dynamite strapped to her chest, and I see him, my age, army sleeves rolled up, put his gun down and reach out to her saying "Honey, honey." He steps forward and his jacket isn't buttoned and he says, "Sweetie. Don't move." She smiles and he sees her white teeth, her dark brown eyes, and he wants to hold her face in his hands, kiss her on the cheeks. Then he sees it before he hears it, watches her break apart then spread out with that awful noise. He's on the ground, his hands over his head and he smells her blowing over him, hears bits of her come down in the trees like rain. I watch him as he throws his gear in the back of the truck, and I try to be him as he climbs in, starts the engine, and backs out fast. I try to feel the shivers that come up my back and neck because I just know the barn is full of gooks, and when I get on the highway I floor it because the faster I move the harder it is for everything and everyone to catch up with me, and even when I slow down to turn off the dirt road to the ranch, I won't be breathing easy enough to know that I've hurt someone at home who loves me.

CHUCK'S STANDING BEHIND the bar, cutting the limes into little wedges, looking up at the TV every few cuts. He's got a good body and it stands out nice in the white short-sleeve shirts Randy makes all the bartenders wear.

"Mornin', Chuck!"

"Hey Sal, how ya doin'?"

"Okay. Is there coffee made up?"

"Nope. I was waiting for you."

"Figures." I walk past the bar into the kitchen and hang up my coat. Jimmy's whistling in the back. "Hi, Jim!"

He sticks his head around the corner. "Oh, good morning there, uh, Sally." He's got his white apron on, stained around the belly from rubbing up against the counter all the time when he's marinating the London broils, making up dips, whipping up the bloody mary mix, and it makes him look skinnier than he is because you expect somebody fat to have that kind of stain across his gut. "We got the punch clock fixed," he says.

"It's about time," I punch in, then make up two pots of coffee, bring one out to the bar. "Where do you want it, Chuck?"

"We got a new hot plate for the coffee drinks. Over there."

I have to walk around to the other side where the customers come in from the parking lot. The bar's long and shaped like a rectangle with the bartenders in the middle. On Saturday nights, when I see everybody dancing so close and crowded up near the band, I wonder why Randy decided to build this huge bar over the old dance floor, and when the bar's full, people standing three deep on all four sides, when Marcie and me have to elbow our way through to shout out our orders, trying not to knock over the empties and dirty glasses on our trays, then I really wonder about having a bar so big. I put the coffeepot down on the hot plate and pour myself some in one of the big clear glasses they use for Irishes. I light a cigarette, then lay it in one of the ashtrays Chuck's got spread out on the bar.

I start on the parking-lot side then move to the street side, flipping the high-backed wooden chairs off the tables, wiping off bits of popcorn and cigarette ash Elaine and Julie always leave behind on their night shifts. I finish the tables just as Jimmy comes from out back with his dirty apron on. He's carrying the green chalkboard we hang in the hallway with the day's specials written on it. "Ready for me yet, Sally?"

"Sure, just a minute," I walk around the bar and get my coffee and cigarette, then come back. He hands me the chalk. "Okay. What're we sellin'?" I ask him.

"Uh, the chicken Maui for four seventy-five. The knockwurst special for two twenty-five . . ."

I write in big clear letters as he talks, putting the food on one side then leaving a space and writing the price on the other. I look at him after each line, see him squint a little as he matches the right price with the right food in his head, then telling me, watching me write it down letter by letter, looking at me while I do it, the way he does whenever we make up the menu together, and it makes me feel special even though I know he does it because I can read and write and he can't.

We finish and I hang up the menu board in the entryway, go back to my coffee, take a big sip, then a drag from my cigarette. I look out the window at the cars going by in the street, the sun getting brighter on them, lunch hour getting close, and I see Rick, standing on the porch in the morning cool, the world gray and brown through the screen behind him: "It's not you babe, it's not you," and my body gives a little, like when you're in an elevator that starts up too fast, and I'm ready just to go lay someplace dark and think, to breathe deep and quiet, to think, and as soon as I let myself begin to feel that, I know the rest of my day's going to be shit, that I won't be able to go through it and believe in it as much, because I've let myself feel something more.

"Hey, Sally, it's after eleven already, babe," Chuck says from the register.

He finishes counting the ones, slapping them into the drawer, closing it, then testing the total button a couple of times quick with his thumb, the drawer sliding out fast and loud and ringing. I put out my cigarette and carry my cup and ashtray out back.

I SHOULD BE ON the bus right now, riding high through the streets, looking out at the city moving by, at all the people dressed in nice clothes standing on the street corners, at the drunk old men curled up against the buildings, their clothes dirtier than the sidewalk, at the old ladies with wrinkled faces that sag into their mouths because they haven't got any teeth, living out of shopping carts filled with old clothes and bags of trash, at the cars that move so close I always think they're going to get sucked under our wheels. Then I would be on the highway looking out at the prairie, at the mountains that sit out there looking so dirty through the haze that comes from all those plants by the tracks, and I'd lay my head back and close my eyes, breathe in that old plastic bus smell, everybody's perfume and cigarette smoke, somebody's gum—and I'd feel my body sink into itself, my arms and legs get heavy with the nap that'd be settling in, then I'd be up with my heart beating, my face feeling thick, heading to the fast air sound of the door, stepping down and out into the air where I'd take a deep breath and start walking up the road where the houses are two and three blocks apart, walk until I'm between being awake and tired again, then onto the porch where I'd smell Lumpy before I saw her, where I'd turn and look out at the mountains before I went in, feeling them behind me like something I can lean against, then into the kitchen where I'd open the refrigerator and look in, feel myself go into a stare, the house quiet, waiting for me to cook in it, waiting for Rick. And when I call Chuck over for my second Seabreeze I know I won't try and catch the four-thirty either, that I'm going to sit here tired from a medium lunch, my body clammy under my skirt, to smoke and drink, to listen to whatever Chuck puts on the system, hoping that it'll be something slow and jazzy, something I can curl up in, like in a dark and quiet place, a place where I can think.

It was our second time together and I woke up first. His room was cool and smelled like old blankets and I could feel his warmth under the covers. I got up and went to the bathroom and I stared at the American flag while I peed. It was old and kind of dirty and he had it nailed to the back of the door. When I got back to the room he was up.

"Get dressed. I'm taking you someplace secret."

We drove up through Rainfall Canyon until we were so high I could see the plains stretched out behind us. I lit us each a cigarette and handed him his as he turned down a dirt road I'd never seen before. He stopped the car and we got out, walked up a narrow muddy trail with brown pine needles on it. I was breathing real hard and I saw him put out his cigarette in his hand, then put it in his jacket pocket. I flicked mine into the woods. We walked until I felt hungry and a little weak, until I wanted a shower before I got close to him again. And I didn't say anything because he was so quiet, his head bent down low all the time except whenever a little animal moved off a branch or something, then he would jerk his head in the direction of the sound, then back again just as quick, like he hadn't meant to look. We came out onto a big flat rock in the sunlight. I stopped and bent over a little, resting my hands on my knees, and he walked ahead of me. I could feel my heart beating in my head and I straightened up, followed him to the edge of the rock.

"Look," he said.

I looked out at the valley, so deep and green, covered with thousands of little trees, the mountains rising up out of it on both sides.

"Do you see it?"

"What?"

"My place."

"What? Where?"

"Look."

I got closer to him and looked down his arm to where he was pointing. I saw trees standing against a short white cliff. "I don't see anything."

He kept his arm pointed straight. "To the left a little."

Then I saw it, a slanted wooden spot that looked kind of gray in the sun.

"What's that?"

"My place." He lowered his arm and looked at me. "You're the only one I've ever showed it to. Even the Rangers don't know anything about it. Least they haven't done anything about it."

"But it looks so lonely. Why out here?"

He looked back out at the valley, at his cabin, then up at the mountains. We could hear the wind blowing through all those trees. He looked down. "I was selling shoes in town, making some good money. One day this gook family comes in, and they weren't Chinese or Korean either, they were gooks, I know. As soon as I saw them I went back to the coffee room. My supervisor was there and I told him that I needed a break and would he please handle the family out front. He told me he was busy and that I could have a break later. The sonuvabitch was having coffee, Sal. Jesus, I don't know what happened, I told him to go fuck himself. He asked me who the hell I thought I was talking to and he got up and shoved me and I knocked him down. I grabbed my jacket and he was calling me a sonuvabitch and I remember seeing blood on my knuckles before I took a deep breath and opened the door, went out front. There was four of them; a man and woman were standing there, so fucking humble-looking, and there was a pretty girl holding her brother's hands so he wouldn't mess with the shoe polish rack. The man smiled and looked like he was about to ask me something, then I could hardly breathe. I saw them all dead. I saw the man and woman's throats cut. I saw the little boy's head lying on his brains in the dirt. His mouth and eyes were still open and his sister was lying next to him, her clothes blown off; her legs were open wide apart and I saw her intestines hanging out all wet and shiny. I got by them and I remember knocking the girl's shoulder. She let out a little shriek and I saw the street outside, the cars moving, the people walking by, and I dove, came down on the sidewalk with all that glass shattering down around me." He stopped and looked at me, looked kind of pale, and I could feel his paleness in me. "When I got out of the hospital I drove me and Rex up here, covered the Buick and trailer with pine, then saddled him up and rode out into that valley. We stayed three months."

"How did you eat?"

"I had my .30-.30. I built that cabin after the first two weeks of freezing my ass off."

I moved closer to him and held his hand, leaned my face into his shoulder and smelled the dampness of his army jacket. He let out a little laugh.

"I've gotten better! It used to be the first thing I'd tell people. 'Hi, how're you? I'm a vet. I get disability for being crazy.' Jesus, I'm getting better." We kissed.

CHUCK COMES AROUND and sits beside me. "You want another?"

"Yeah, okay." I slide my glass towards him but he calls Larry and I look up, see Larry's gold chain, his smooth and always shaved face.

"What're you, workin' a double, Sal?"

"Oh hi, Larry. I didn't see you. I'll have another one of these please." I hold up my glass.

"Just relaxing tonight, huh Sally?"

"You got it."

"I'll take a Bud, pal," Chuck says. He turns to me. "So what's the matter?"

"Why should anything be the matter? I'm just sitting here having a few drinks is all."

"Yeah? Then why do you look so shitty?"

"Thanks."

Larry brings us our drinks and Chuck pays him in ones, leaving him a dollar for a tip. We clink our glasses together and Chuck finishes his off all at once while I sip off mine, tasting more vodka than cranberry and grapefruit. He raises his hand to Larry for another.

"Hard day, Chuck?"

"Catch-up time, darlin', catch-up time."

I look straight ahead over the bar and out the window, at a man and woman getting out of their car, at the woman's yellow top standing out bright in the late afternoon gray. "Chuck, you ever feel like, like you're just not good enough?"

He sips from his new beer, thinking about it.

"I mean like all day and all night? Even on your days off?"

"No." He looks at me. "Do you?"

I take a deep drag off my cigarette and turn away from him. He asks me again, but I know if I talk I'll cry. I put out my cigarette and suck my drink through the straw until it makes that liquid sucking sound in the ice.

"Hey, Sal." He touches my shoulder. "How're you and Mr. Rick doing these days?"

I turn to him and hold up my empty glass. Larry brings us our drinks, but he doesn't stop to talk. I watch how fast he's moving back there, his gold chain swinging over the beer cooler, and then I know he's been moving that way for a while now. I look around at all the people that have come in, hear their loud talk and laughing and it's like somebody just turned up the sound to a show I hadn't been watching. And so I watch them, look at the young business-men with their jackets that match their ties that match their shirts that match their shoes, laugh with their mouths open so wide, holding their Glenlivets and Tanqueray tonics, so fucking sure of themselves, and I know if I was working they'd be patting my ass and leaving a quarter tip for a twenty-dollar tab. I look across the bar at two girls who come in here a lot, always so dressed up because they type and run for coffee at one of those law offices up the street. They wear these white blouses with little pretty ties and tight flannel jackets that go halfway down their skirts, and they think they're so fucking important with their briefcases full of other people's work, talking to me and Marcie like we were born just to bring them their lousy white wines and brandies. And then I see Larry's gold chain swinging over the beer cooler again, see him smiling and sweating for all these assholes, trying to make a living, and I feel that part of me come out that always comes out when I'm around people when I shouldn't be, the part that hates, that wants the soft humming in my head to get so loud that it blends in with all the noise in the room, so I can look at them all without thinking about how much they make me think the world's going to end because everybody sucks so much, until I can sink back into the voices and clinking glasses and music like that's all there is, until I'm numb. I lift my drink to my lips and like how my arm works without my telling it to. I look at Chuck. "Rick's a fucking asshole."

HE'S GOT ME UP against the car, his tongue thick and cold from the beer, and the door handle's digging into my back. I pull away.

"What's the matter?" he says.

"Nothing." I kiss him quick on the cheek. "Let's go." I walk around the back of the car and balance myself against the roof while he unlocks the door from the inside. I get in and he kisses me again, pulls me into it with his hand behind my head, the other one pressing against my breast through my clothes. We stop and I lean back against the window, my head heavy on my shoulders, and watch the green glow of the lights above his lap.

I'm out of cigarettes and I ask him to stop at a 7-Eleven before we get on the highway. He turns and parks in front of a doughnut shop, leans over and slides his hand under my skirt, squeezes my leg. "I'll use the machine. Be right back."

I press down on his hand with mine, liking how cool it feels, and I tell him to hurry. He only has AM on the radio. I play with the dial, but I get talk shows and flick it off. I look at Chuck through the glass, watch him getting change, and I see how wide his back and shoulders look compared to his ass, see how the bright light brings out the blond in his hair and I want him to hurry up, to give me my cigarettes and buy us some beer, to get us out of the city with all of its fake light, to hit the highway where it's dark and go real real fast, and if the radio won't work, then we'll sing something and fill up the quiet of the car with our sounds.

He gets in and hands me my cigarettes.

"Let's get something to drink," I say.

"I've got plenty at my place." He leans over and kisses me hard and I kiss too, pulling my head back a little to keep his tongue from going deep, feeling strange about not thinking about where we were going.

"Can't we just drive somewhere?"

He looks at me kind of confused, then smiles. "Yeah, sure, I know where we can go."

We get on the highway with nothing to drink and I sit closer to him. He puts his arm around me and I rub his stomach under his shirt, undo one of the buttons and scratch his hair. He kisses the top of my head and I can hear his heart beat in his chest. I sit up and light a cigarette. I don't offer him one and look out the window at the night, see the lights on in the ugly square houses near the highway. I pass them every day on the bus, look at their little fenced-in yards with the little round plastic swimming pools and rusted metal swing sets, the grass all dry and yellow, worn down to dirt in some places.

"Hey babe, c'mere." He puts his arm around me again and pulls me closer. I can smell the bar on him and ignore it, lick his ear and scratch the back of his head under the hair.

He turns off the highway and drives down a street lit up on both sides with the light from gas stations and all-night stores. I take a drag from my cigarette and put it to his mouth and we smoke it together until it's gone, his arm around me, squeezing my breast through my jacket. We're on a street with no streetlights and not many houses either. He stops in front of an empty place between two houses, a little grassy field I can just see the beginning of, it's gotten so dark. He turns off the car and is on me with both hands. He twists himself away from the steering wheel and we go down onto the seat. His whiskers burn my face and we kiss long and deep, my hands pulling on his back. He moves against my legs and I can feel him through his pants. I arch my head back away from his face.

"Let's go outside," he says into my ear. "I've got a blanket."

"Okay."

He's off of me and I hear him outside moving things around in his trunk. I remember waking up late for school. Mama, she used to make me walk, and right before I got there, when I could see the red brick building through the trees, I'd turn and go down the street to Danny's Donuts, sit there for hours making two cups of coffee last the rest of the day, never having said to myself that that's what I was going to do, letting my body decide, letting it take me out of my life. I get out and close the door real soft. I breathe deep through my nose and smell fresh-cut grass and motor oil. My mouth is dry and wants something cold and sweet. He closes the trunk and comes over to me with a blanket over his shoulder, I can't see his face but I can feel the smile.

I slip off my shoes and lie down on his blanket. I hear the zipper and hold up my arms. He finds them and lies beside me, his legs hairy and warm against mine. He moves his hand under my skirt and touches me over my underpants. I lift up a little so he can pull them down. He gets them past my knees and I sit up and pull them down and over my feet. I lie back against his arm. He leans down and kisses my open mouth, his tongue sliding over my teeth, then down deep. He pulls my skirt up over my hips and I help him with one hand. I'm breathing fast and I reach down and hold him there, feel his heart beating in it, warm and hard; I spread my legs beneath him and he holds himself over me with his arms straight, everything tingles and I rub it around the outside first, leaving my wetness on him. He pushes forward and I guide him in, then reach my hand around his back. I close my eyes and let my feet come off the blanket as he pushes all the way, opens me up. I hold him tight, feel the muscles move in his back, and I let my body move with his, feel the ground against the back of my head, everything's dark, and there's Ricky, hopping alongside Rex with one foot in the stirrup then pushing off and swinging his leg over as he comes down in the saddle. They're moving, Rex's tail jerking black and shiny in the sun; they jump the fence and come down together in one motion, moving fast out into the plains, heading for the mountains, Rick's shirt rippling in the wind, moving faster and faster, jumping over some brush then coming down hard without stopping, going into the shadow of the mountains. He pulls his rifle out from somewhere in front of him then raises it with one arm to his shoulder and fires at the hills five times fast, the barrel jumping up each time, making a hollow cracking sound, little puffs of white smoke hanging in the air behind them. He lowers it then flings it out away from him into the weed, bends low over the saddle, his face almost rubbing against Rex's neck, then kicks into his sides with his boots. They move into darker shadows and I see his hat flip off his head, hang in the air for a second, then drop. I open my eyes wide to the darkness, to Chuck's grunting, his mouth wet on my throat, and I'm holding him tight, moving with him, moving, feeling him shudder as the first little wave of heat fills me. I hold him tighter and look up at the sky.

WHITE TREES,
HAMMER MOON

It was only a three-hour ride north to the White Mountains of New Hampshire but until today had begun Rory Enfield had worried about it, had worried that if this time in the cab of his pickup was bad, that if they were all quiet with each other and didn't know what to say, or if the two kids weren't getting along and he had to settle something, then the whole weekend would collapse on itself before it ever got going. But driving up the sunlit highway with April sitting between him and Vinnie, the three of them talking loose and relaxed about whatever came up—about nine-year-old April having made a banana cake at school, about Vinnie's friend Mark being thirteen like him but with a minibike already—Rory felt both silly and relieved; he should've known: kids adjust, grown people don't. And this morning he'd take what he could get. Right now it was good just sharing the same air as the two stepchildren he wouldn't see for a long time. Be thankful for small things, he told himself. Be glad you're alive at all.

It was twelve-thirty when they came to the first tree-covered slopes of the mountains. They were all hungry so Rory stopped off at The General Store in Woodstock and bought a smoked sausage and cheddar cheese, sour pickles, a loaf of french bread, a bag of chocolate chip cookies, and three Cokes in green glass bottles. Behind the store were some picnic tables under the pines. They sat at one and ate.

Rory cut some sausage for April with his fold-out Puma knife, but she didn't seem to notice. She pinched off a piece of cheese then put it on a cookie. Rory sipped his Coke and watched Vinnie make himself a sausage and pickle sub. It was huge, about half the loaf and half the meat.

"You eat all that you'll get cramps on the hike."

"How long is it, Daddy?" April studied her cheese and cookie sandwich, then ate it.

Rory scratched his beard. "Five miles."

"*Five?* Wow."

"Yeah so take it slow, okay big man?"

Vinnie nodded then swallowed.

The air was cool and Rory could smell pine pitch. May in the White Mountains was nothing to fool with, he knew. He zipped up his motorcycle jacket. "Where's your sweaters?"

"In Vinnie's pack."

"I think you'll want 'em tonight." He leaned over and kissed April on the top of her head. Her braided blond hair smelled clean and a little like cherries.

"I'm getting a coffee for the road. You guys clean up and I'll meet you at the truck."

THE RIDE TO CRAWFORD NOTCH took another hour but nobody seemed to be counting the minutes. At first the road was very narrow with tall evergreens on both sides; Rory pointed out which was which as they drove by. Most were eastern white pines, he said, but there were some black spruce and jack pines too. He told them how a lot of other carpenters don't know about trees but he thought they should. It's like a butcher not knowing anything about cows or pigs. He took the truck around a curve and up a long hill. When the road began to level again, there were no trees to the left, just the sky and the rounded peaks of mountains rising out of a wide valley that seemed to go on for miles. Rory rolled his window down and rested his elbow outside. Vinnie did the same.

At Franconia, they left 93 for route 302 that cut east through the national forest. For thirteen miles the road dipped, climbed, and curved. Around Breton Woods, on Vinnie's side, they could see the white-water river that led to Arethusa Falls.

Rory pointed his thumb out his window. "Take a look."

"What?" Vinnie said.

"Yeah, what?"

"Mount Washington."

"That big one with the snow all over the top?" April put her hands on his leg as she turned and looked out the cab's rear window.

"That's it."

"It's not that big, Rory. Mount Everest is big."

Rory glanced past April at Vinnie. He'd never heard that

before; what was this "Rory" shit? Vinnie was looking out the back window at the mountain. There was hurt in his face, that, and some kind of vague fuck you. Rory wanted to mention how the wind can blow up to two hundred miles an hour up there. He didn't want to talk about anything else: "I'd appreciate it if you didn't call me that, Vin."

"What?"

"Yeah, what?" April said as she sat back down and looked straight ahead.

"Rory."

"That's your name, isn't it?"

"Right."

"I don't like that name, Dad."

"See Vin, she calls me Dad. Grown people call me Rory; your mom calls me that. I've been with you kids since April knew only about fifty words. You can call me what you used to."

Vinnie sort of half nodded but he didn't say anything.

They were quiet for almost a mile and Rory was beginning to wonder if he'd said something harder than he thought he had. They passed a Deer Crossing sign. April read it out loud and started talking about Bambi and mean hunters. Thank God for April, Rory thought. Sweet April.

There was only one car in the parking area of the Crawford Notch Trails. It was a white Toyota with an I Brake for Animals sticker on its rear bumper. Rory could picture the owner, probably some skinny carrot-eating bastard who didn't smoke or drink and sipped tea after a long hike alone. He pulled the truck up close to the opening of the trails.

"Which camp are we going to?"

"Wild Birch."

"That sign says seven miles, not five."

"I know it, Vin. I didn't want to scare you off."

"Yeah sure." Vinnie opened his door and got out of the truck. "I can walk a hundred miles easy."

"No you can't. Nobody can walk a hundred miles, can they Dad?"

Rory held the door for April. He walked around the truck and let down the tailgate. Vinnie was already standing in the bed of the pickup. He had his nylon pack on and held a rolled sleeping bag beneath each arm. He was breathing hard but was trying to hide it by keeping his mouth shut.

"Slow down, buddy. I know you're strong, but we have to pack ourselves right for the walk."

"Can they?" April was standing beside Rory looking up at him.

"Some people can."

"Like Mick Welch."

"That ugly man you live with, Dad?"

"Hey Vinnie, Mick doesn't walk anywhere he can bike. When him and his wife go food shopping he rides his Harley right into the store up and down the aisles. Marie just sits behind him and grabs what she can."

"Really, Dad?"

Rory smiled down at April, then winked at Vinnie. Vinnie looked away and hopped out of the truck.

The dirt trail was wide and hard-packed. For the first mile it was flat and cut through a short section of woods, then a grassy field. The sun was at its highest point and Rory didn't think it was quite sixty-five degrees. The kids were walking ahead of him. First Vinnie, then April. She had wanted to carry more than just her bag of marshmallows so Rory had strapped her sleeping bag to her back with his belt. He tied a knot, and when he cinched it in, she smiled and said it was like they were all soldiers in a war or something. Vinnie was still carrying his sleeping bag, their own little pack, plus his canteen of water. Rory'd told him it was all too much, that he would get tired after a mile or two, but he was glad the boy was doing it; Mick's camping gear probably weighed seventy or eighty pounds at least, and Rory didn't think he could carry more than he already was.

The tent was rolled tight and strapped high into the aluminum frame. His sleeping bag was tied at the bottom, beneath the pack, but inside was Rory's big mistake: the food. He should have listened to Mick and Marie and gotten the light freeze-dried stuff, but he hadn't. He went out and bought two family-sized cans of beans and franks, a loaf of Wonder Bread, a jar of mustard, some peanut butter, a box of oatmeal, a brick of american cheese, ten Almond Joy bars, a jar of instant coffee, a bottle of A-1 sauce, three wrapped frozen steaks, and one aluminum cooking pot. Then, early this morning, after driving down to the Merrimack Police Station to piss in a jar for the desk sergeant, he went back to the Welches and filled his double-sized flask with half a fifth of Jack Daniel's. He knew the JD was a Monday morning risk, that traces of it would stay in his blood, but so what? he'd thought. What can they do now they haven't already done? He'd dropped the flask into the pack along with two sixteen-ounce Coors, then he drove to his old trailer and picked up the kids.

This pack, shit. Every time Rory stepped downward the tent nudged the back of his head and he felt like he was going to fall on his face. When the trail rose and he had to climb, the bottom rung of the frame pushed into his butt and he would have to bend forward to ease it up. Seven miles. He felt pretty dumb about that.

Mick had told him it was a fin and not too steep. He was right about the second part. The trail wasn't climbing or falling really. It seemed to be going along the spine of a ridge. Whenever there was a break in the trees they could see a shallow valley to their left, and a deeper, wider one to the right. It was padded green with Canada hemlocks and an occasional birch. After the first half hour of walking, the trail became smooth slabs of granite and April slipped and fell forward on her hands and knees. Rory noticed her shoes. She wasn't wearing shit-kicker boots with deep treads like her brother. She had pink sneakers on her feet with smooth green soles. He caught up to her and started to squat down but she picked up the bag of marshmallows, smiled at him, and was walking again before he could straighten up under his pack. She followed Vinnie who disappeared as the trail dipped and went into a thicket of white cedars.

Rory was breathing hard and the pack's straps were digging into his shoulder muscles. Fucking Alene. She can't tell the little girl she's got to wear her boots? Jesus. His eyes began to burn. He pulled his bandana from his leather jacket pocket and wiped his forehead. The jacket was too much. When they stopped for a break, he was going to take it off and tie it into the pack somehow. He followed the trail into the trees. It went to the right and climbed again. The air was cooler here and the sun came through in patches. There were granite chunks in the hill that Rory used as steps all the way to the top. He expected to see the kids then but he didn't. The path dropped again and was very rocky. He started down and grabbed the trees beside the trail to balance himself. He was stepping down and over the rocks very quickly and when the ground leveled and the thicket became a clearing, he was walking as fast as he could under the pack's weight. Then he saw them.

Down off the trail to the right, they were both standing on a flat rock looking out at Crawford Notch.

"Hey." He was breathing so hard he didn't know if he'd just said something or not. He started to lean over to rest his hands on his knees but the pack was too heavy. He straightened, slipped it off his shoulders, and set it down in the middle of the trail. A wind was blowing south from the ridge across the valley. It dried the sweat on his face and blew easily through his beard. He thought how the kids should be wearing their sweaters. He started for the rock but stopped at the edge of the trail. When would he see them like this again? They were both standing perfectly still. Vinnie stood close to the edge while April stayed back a few feet. Rory didn't know if they were staring out at the earth or the sky. The earth was something. The Crotch, Mick'd called it. More beautiful than any woman's you ever been in. But it was more than that, Rory thought as he gazed past April and Vinnie at Crawford Notch, where the ridge across the valley and the ridge they were on come together. Land joining land. From a plane it must look like a big green horseshoe. And where the ridges meet, the valley looked to be at its deepest point. That's where the camp was supposed to be, nestled in a basin of paper birches.

April pointed to the sky above the Notch. There was a towering wall of white clouds that dissipated and curved over the top like a wave. Rory opened the pack, took out three candy bars, and walked down to the flat rock.

"Daddy *look*, isn't the sky beautiful?"

"Yeah, it is."

Vinnie glanced at Rory. His eyes were watery from the wind. "Spare some water?"

Vinnie handed over the canteen. It held a quart of liquid and had a blue nylon cover with a long adjustable strap.

"This new?"

Vinnie nodded.

"Dougie gave it to him. He bought us flashlights too."

Rory let that one sink in a second, then he concentrated on holding the canteen for April to drink from. He didn't care how many toys "Dougie" had bought the kids; he wasn't along on this trip. Out here, Doug Cohen did not exist.

When April finished, Rory drank. Then he looked at Vinnie looking out at the valley. He reached into his jacket pocket for one of the candy bars. "Catch."

Rory tossed it just as Vinnie turned around. It glanced off the boy's shoulder, hit the rock, then slid down it and off.

"Oops."

"That's pollution, you know."

"Sorry, man. My fault." Rory gave April an Almond Joy then stood and held the third one out to Vinnie.

"Don't want it."

"Give you energy. We got a ways to go."

"You eat it, Daddy. It's good."

Rory squatted next to April. She was sitting down cross-legged and one of her blond braids was resting on the sleeping bag at her back.

"That too tight?"

She shook her head as she chewed.

"How long are we gonna stay here?"

"Relax, buddy. We're taking a short rest."

Vinnie put down his rolled sleeping bag and sat on it. Rory swallowed chocolate and coconut and watched the boy, wondered where things'd gone wrong with him. He was fine until they got to the mountains. He seemed to be okay when they stopped to eat even. Maybe it was the kid's balls, he thought. Thirteen years old.

Maybe his hormones are already starting the Yo-Yo Jitterbug, the Everything's Fine–Everything Sucks Blues. Or maybe it was this weekend.

"Dad. Do you think heaven looks like that cloud?"

"I don't know, sweets."

"Somebody knows." Vinnie was looking down at his feet when he said it.

"'Scuse me, Vin. What'd you say?"

"Nothin'."

"No. You said something, now what was it?"

Vinnie's eyes were still wet. He looked like he was about to shout something, but then he glanced back down at his feet. "I said somebody knows, that's all."

"Knows what?"

"What heaven looks like."

"He means God, Dad."

"Yeah, *God*." Vinnie got up and walked past them to the trail.

Rory took a breath and let it out. He knew what Vinnie was talking about. April did too. But he wouldn't talk about it now. Not like this. "Before you go off, you take your sister's sweater out of that pack and give it to her."

"I'm not cold, Dad."

"You will be, hon. Trust me."

THE REST OF THE HIKE was downhill into the valley and the kids were taking it fast, but Rory went slow. He had tied his motorcycle jacket across the top of Vinnie's pack and for a while he kept his eyes on that; watching his leather jerk and sway as Vinnie scurried down the trail seemed to help. It set the beat in his head. He didn't think so much about how shaky hot and gorged with blood his thigh muscles felt, how they seemed to be working on their own now and that if the trail leveled or climbed again, his legs would keep walking even if he didn't want them to. Then he couldn't see Vinnie anymore. He was moving too fast. Now it was April he watched, her blond pigtails bobbing along. Her sleeping bag was still tied snug against her and she carried the bag of marshmallows in her left hand.

This was a good hike. It felt to Rory like roofing does when you really get into the groove, when you've tacked all your plywood sheets into place on the rafters and it's nailing time. The sun's out but not too hot. There's a bandana around your head for the sweat. You're working alone, but in your right hand is your long-handled framing hammer, and hanging at your waist is an apron full of nails. You grab six or seven galvanized then start from the ridge and work down. At first you drive them in four swings, then three. When you're cooking, it's *bap-bap,* the nail's buried in two. It's not finish work, but still, you're not leaving any hammer moons on the wood. And the fingers of your left hand are magic. They're setting up the next nail while you're still pounding the one before it, so you never stop, you never even pause. You finish nailing the eleventh sheet of plywood, straighten, drop your hammer into its belt hook, then take one breath, maybe two before you climb over the ridge and start the other side.

Alene used to like all that, Rory was sure. When he'd built that bedroom addition for her uncle, she said she got juiced just watching Rory sweat and swing his hammer like it was a part of his body, his thoughts even. The last day of the job, when he had to finish painting the clapboard siding, she'd helped him. It was cool and cloudy and Rory had worried about rain. But she showed up at ten that morning with two coffees and three honey-dipped doughnuts. She had her blond hair tied up in a scarf. She wore paint-splattered work boots, jeans ripped at both knees, and a blue sleeveless workshirt that she'd tied off at the waist. Through the shirt holes beneath her armpits, Rory could see the pale outward curve of her breasts. He hooked his finger inside, pulled the shirt back, and kissed her nipple until she pushed him away laughing.

They were done by three. She went in to wash up and leave her uncle a note, then they got on Rory's Harley and cruised the wind to The Hideaway Lounge. There were only a couple customers at the bar, two sheetrockers Rory didn't know. He ordered two cold Buds from skinny Pete then carried them back to the table between the jukebox and the dartboard. Alene'd punched in some songs already, slow ones they could hold each other to: Patsy Cline, Stevie Nicks, some old Springsteen. They were pressing close together and Bruce was singing "Jersey Girl" when Rory said it; he leaned back, lifted her chin with two fingers, and looked into her face. "Let's just do it, Alene."

"Here, Rore? They'll all watch us."

He shook his head once. "Your kids need a daddy. And Lord knows I sure's shit need you."

She stopped smiling, and in the midafternoon dark of the barroom her eyes seemed to get more round. Her eyes began to well up. Then she wrapped her arms around his neck and kissed him, her tongue darting around inside his mouth like she was looking for what part of him to thank for all this.

They didn't finish their beers. They rode home just as it started to rain. When they got to Rory's trailer, the rain was really whipping down but he didn't cover his Harley. He unlocked the door for Alene and when he stepped in after her, she already had her workshirt off. She moved to him and pulled his T-shirt over his head and arms. They kissed, then pulled away from each other to untie and pull off their boots. When she unsnapped his jeans and he unzipped hers, they were both laughing. She stood naked in front of him, her hair dripping. She stopped smiling and her eyes got that round look again. She stepped closer and wrapped her arms around his neck. He put his hands beneath her butt and lifted her to him. The rain was coming down so hard on the tin roof of the trailer, it was all they could hear.

The trail was rockier than ever, but Rory was walking fast enough to stay ten or fifteen feet behind April, twenty or thirty behind her brother. They were on flat ground now and were moving toward the foot of Crawford Notch. The air was cool, in the high fifties, Rory figured. He thought he should be wearing his jacket to keep from getting a chill. He thought about Vinnie not wearing his sweater, just an Iron Maiden T-shirt that he didn't have tucked in. He wished again April had worn boots and heavy socks.

Then they were in it, the thickest birch grove Rory'd ever seen. On both sides of the trail, as deep as he could see, were white trees. Some were still beginning to sprout buds but most were leafed out already. The trail was smooth here, and along its sides were wide green ferns. Up ahead, April stopped and waited for him. Rory dug his thumbs in between his shoulders and the pack's straps and walked faster. When he was close to her, she was smiling, pointing into the birches.

"I saw a movie in school? About a cave that elephants go to to die, or that their elephant friends drag them to? It looked just like that, Dad. Like a forest of bones."

"But it's pretty, isn't it?"

April nodded. Back at the flat rock her cheeks had been flushed, but now they looked strangely pale. He put his palm to her forehead.

"You're too dry. You all right?"

"I'm thirsty."

"Course you are. We've been walking hard." Rory looked past her down the trail and called out to Vinnie. The boy's voice came back through the trees.

"I'm *here!* There's a *stream too!*"

The Wild Birch Camp was a small dirt clearing in the trees. There was an empty iron garbage barrel chained to the trunk of a skinny hackberry. In front of the clearing was a dry bed of small rocks, then a stream that flowed back in the direction from which they'd come. The water was flowing fast, foaming and spilling over granite boulders. It was loud and Rory was surprised he hadn't heard it back on the trail. He watched Vinnie get down on his hands and knees and drink. On the other side was the steep rise of Crawford Notch. The sun was already behind it. A huge shadow fell over the camp.

"It's like a giant wall, isn't it Daddy?"

"Absolutely." Rory squatted and slipped off the pack. When he stood, his upper body went light, but his neck and shoulders felt like they were being pinched by a steel clamp. He untied April's sleeping bag from her back. He picked up the canteen and held it for her while she drank. There was no sweat on her forehead or upper lip. None. That worried him. He wasn't sure what it was called when that happened, but he knew it wasn't good. He put his belt on and strapped the Puma knife and sheath to his side. When April lowered the canteen, he fastened the top button of her sweater.

"I'm hot."

"Here. Sit on your sleeping bag and rest. Me and your brother are gonna set up camp."

The hike seemed to have helped Vinnie. He was walking around with more energy than Rory'd seen in him all day. It was like April's and a part of Rory's had gone into the boy. And he was taking orders well. When Rory asked him to pick up the loose twigs and rocks where they were going to make camp, he had the space cleared before Rory'd even untied the tent. He unrolled the yellow canvas so the doorway would face the water and the Notch. They started from the bottom and worked to the top. Vinnie threaded each of the five base poles through the canvas loops in the tent's roof. While he was doing that, Rory worked the upper pole sections through to meet the lower ones. He had Vinnie hold them together while he screwed them in tight. There was a special clip that held all five poles together at the top center of the tent, but Rory didn't see it anywhere. He checked the small outer pockets of the pack, then he laid it on its side and gently shook out the food. One of the family-sized cans of beans and franks rolled onto the Wonder Bread loaf and stayed there. April nudged it off with her foot. Rory smelled steak sauce, lots of it. Then he saw its brown smear all over the box of oatmeal. There was some on the peanut butter jar, a dab on one of the Coors beers, but most of it was inside the pack. "Damn."

"What's the matter, Dad?"

"Nothin', sweetie. The steak sauce spilled, that's all."

"Oh."

The empty A-1 bottle rolled out last. At least it wasn't broken. Rory turned the pack upside down and shook it. No clip.

"My arm's getting tired over here." Vinnie was leaning over the tent, holding all five poles together with two hands.

"Want some water, Dad?"

Rory shook his head, then glanced back at the canteen's long adjustable strap. It hung over April's wrist and touched her knee. He took the canteen from her, flicked open his knife, and cut off the strap.

"*Hey,* that's brand-new."

"Sorry, Vin. I didn't think." Rory stepped to the edge of the tent and worked the strap through the eye of all five poles, then he cinched it in tight and tied it off with a bolin knot. "You gotta be flexible when you build things, buddy. I'll buy you a new canteen."

"What, in a year? No thanks."

"It looks like a yellow igloo, you guys."

"Hey Vin, don't eat yellow snow."

Vinnie didn't smile. He grabbed his pack and sleeping bag and crawled into the tent.

Rory picked his motorcycle jacket up off the rocks and put it on. He pulled a bandana from one of the pockets, then he squatted and began to wipe the A-1 sauce from the Skippy jar. "I guess we'll have to put peanut butter on our steaks tonight."

April didn't laugh. He glanced up at her. She wasn't even smiling. She had her palms clasped between her legs and was looking out at the stream. Rory touched her forehead and cheek. He grabbed her sleeping bag and took her hand.

"I want you to lie down awhile, okay?"

Inside the tent, Vinnie had his sleeping bag rolled out against the north wall. He was lying on his back with his hands clasped behind his head, looking up at the canvas ceiling.

"Your sister's not feeling so good, Vin. Help her get into her sleeping bag. I'm going to gather up some firewood while I can still see it. Come help me after."

Outside, Rory untied his sleeping bag from the frame. He finished wiping the steak sauce off everything, then he carried the empty pack down to the stream and dipped it in against the current. The water felt so cold against his wrists he was surprised there wasn't any ice formed around the rocks or at the edge of the stream. After he rinsed out the pack and shook off the excess water, he laid it over the garbage barrel near the hackberry tree. It was already too dark in the birches to see much, and he figured any wood he'd find under the ferns would be too wet. He glanced at the tent, picked up the flask, and headed for the stream.

He stepped over rocks and made it to the other side without getting water on his boots. He couldn't believe how dark it'd gotten. It's the Notch, he thought. There's probably more sunlight on the other side. In the meadow before it, ten yards downstream, was a fallen shagbark hickory. Rory set his flask down and wondered how, with all the higher trees around, lightning had picked this one. He kicked a long dry limb off the trunk, braced one end over his shoulder, the other on the ground, then stomped on its middle and broke it in half.

He started making a pile for him and Vinnie to carry back to the camp. April had felt too hot, he knew that. He'd build a fire close to the tent to cook over and he'd make April drink three canteens of water, stay in her sleeping bag. When he first touched her face, he thought she'd just walked too hard and needed to rest. But then her cheeks had felt feverish and her eyes got that dark but distant look people get when their world starts to look unworldly. He wished he'd brought some aspirin. Band-Aids too. He picked up the flask and felt the liquid promise of it in his hand. He uncapped it, passed the opening under his nose, then took a short hit: oh Jesus Mary and Saint Joseph's what a treat. The Big Man's own elixir. A ten-month drought ended. A fat check cashed. Rory just knew the center of the earth was filled with the stuff. He gathered an armful of wood and started back over the rocks he could see. Just before he reached the other side, his left foot slipped into the water and a light beam shone into his face. "Who the fuck is that?"

"Me." Vinnie lowered the flashlight. He had put on a heavy wool sweater and was eating a candy bar.

"Oh. I forgot you had a light."

"Doug gave it to me."

"That's right too. It's good you brought it, Vin. All I got is a lighter."

Rory dropped the wood on the ground near the tent. "Man, the sun turned in early, didn't it? I can hardly see your face."

"April's sick."

"I know it."

"Mom had the flu last week."

"Good."

"Good?"

"I mean it's good April's got the flu instead of heatstroke, or sunstroke, or whatever you call it. I was worried about her not sweating."

"She never sweats."

"Give me your flashlight. I want to check on her."

"She's got her own."

Rory couldn't see if Vinnie was smiling or not. He could only see the vague outline of the boy's head and shoulders, the white of the birches behind him.

"Can I do the fire?"

Rory reached into his jeans pocket for his Bic lighter. It was still in the silver sheath Alene'd given him on their seventh anniversary, just a few months before nursing school and Doug Cohen. Beneath the sculpted figure of a bearded man on a horse were the words *Even long riders need somebody. I love you. A.*

Rory handed it to Vinnie. "Don't lose that."

"I *won't.*"

Rory stuck his head inside the tent. April was lying in her sleeping bag. Her flashlight was on the ground near her head lighting up the yellow canvas wall behind her. Her eyes were closed; she looked like she was asleep.

While Vinnie started the fire, Rory took his flashlight and headed back over the stream for more wood. He wedged the butt of the light into the ground so he could see. The hickory must've been down for a while; the upper branches were breaking easily from the trunk. He thought how lucky they were the wood was this dry, but the farther down the tree he worked the thicker the branches were and he wished he'd brought along a hatchet. By using all his weight, he could still pull the limbs free, but now, to break them in half, he had to lean them against the main trunk and jump with both feet on the center of the branch. The first one cracked cleanly in half, and the second and the third, but on the fourth branch Rory slipped and came down on his butt. The metal flask pushed flat and hard against him. He reached around and pulled it from his pocket.

On the other side of the stream, Vinnie had the fire going. He had stacked the wood end-to-end to form a pyramid, and the flames were licking in and around the base of the logs. For a minute, Rory didn't know who he was looking at. The kid with the wool sweater on standing by the fire did not look like a kid; he looked like a short clean-shaven man. Rory swung his legs off the branch and leaned back against the main trunk. He uncapped the flask, drank from it, and glanced at the six sections of broken tree on the ground to his left. They had snapped under him like nothing, like they'd been waiting all fall and winter for him to come along in his steel-toed boots and hundred-eighty-five-pound body to do just that, to finish what a bolt of lightning had already started, to break them up and burn them back to dust.

Like Cohen finishing off him and Alene, though even now, right this minute, Rory had to admit he still had a hard time believing what this past year'd shown him, that as a twosome he and Alene had definitely run out of juice. Looking back, there were signs he could have noticed. She did drop a smoke grenade here and there. The first seemed minor, but it was the jab before two more jabs before the right cross to the nose. She told him he'd look better if he shaved his beard and just kept his moustache. Not more handsome, but better. Then she stopped wanting to go on Sunday Harley runs from barroom to barroom with Mick and Marie. She said it was boring. She had nothing to talk about with Marie, and everybody drank too much. She'd rather stay home with the kids. Then this: one night she actually asked him to sell his hog, to trade it in for the down payment on a nice car so when they all went out as a family, they wouldn't have to squeeze into the cab of his pickup, and she wouldn't feel silly putting on mascara only to sit in a truck with loose nails rolling around her feet.

Rory sipped from the flask. Until the wipeout last July, things were going okay. He drove around Merrimack and Amesbury and Haverhill. He'd bid on one- or two-man building jobs. He'd get them, lay out plans, order stock, then do what he could. At night he went straight home to his trailer, Alene, and the kids. Four or five nights a week, after eating something Alene'd cooked—ham and beans usually, or spaghetti with meat sauce—he'd kick start his scoot and ride the tar to The Hideaway Lounge for a few beers, a couple blackberry brandies. Sometimes, if the girl next door could come and sit, Alene'd ride with him, would hug his gut all the way down windy 110. Then it's summer. Alene's going to nursing school three nights a week and one Wednesday she comes home an hour early, her face drawn and smoking Merit after Merit, to say that she's in love with a nurse named Doug and this guy Doug is what I really need in a man. Not you, Rory, not you.

The JD wasn't going down smooth at all. Not like good stuff should. Instead of a warm slow seeping, it seemed to be kicking its way down his throat. And the buzz felt wrong; it was coming too fast, after only a few shots, and it wasn't rounding out any of the sharp edges. It was somehow leaving everything ragged. The flames of Vinnie's fire were almost as high as the tent, but Rory didn't see Vinnie anywhere. He put away the flask, gathered up the hickory, and waded shin-deep through the stream to the camp. He dropped the wood near the tent and crawled inside.

The rear wall was still lit up by April's flashlight. She was on her hands and knees and Vinnie was kneeling beside her holding her forehead with two hands. Rory could smell the vomit as he crawled up beside Vinnie. Just as he got there April retched twice. When she was done she began to cry. Rory took out his bandana and reached past Vinnie to wipe her mouth. She turned her head away and dry-heaved.

"It's still got steak sauce on it, Rory."

Rory tossed the bandana into the corner. He rested his palm on April's back and patted gently.

"You smell like whiskey, you know."

Vinnie was looking at him, but Rory couldn't see much of his face. "How's that any of your damned business, Vin?"

The boy turned and crawled fast out of the tent. April was crying again. Softly, though, like she didn't want anyone to hear her. She sat back on her calves and wiped her mouth with her hands.

"I'm sorry you're sick, sweetie."

She sniffled and nodded her head.

"Come lay on your brother's sleeping bag while I clean up."

"Do we have any Coke?"

"No, hon, just water. I'll get it."

The fire was huge and Vinnie was dropping the last of the six logs into it.

"The fuck're you *do*in'?" Rory reached into the flames and grabbed the log Vinnie'd just dropped in. With his boot he nudged out three more and kicked them onto the bed of rocks near the stream. Smoke rose from all three and one of them was burning.

"Your sister's got a fever and you're doin' this. Nice."

"Oh screw you."

Rory stood very still. Like doing that would allow those three words to fly past him and get lost in the woods. An accidental discharge. A simple mistake. But standing still wasn't working. Vinnie was looking right at him and what he said hung between them like a still-raised fist that'd just sucker punched Rory. He was on the boy before he knew he'd moved. He gripped Vinnie's sweater in his fists, pushed him back, then jerked him close so their faces were almost touching.

"Listen you little turd. Nobody talks like that to me. Especially you." Rory pushed him back and let go. Vinnie half waved his arms to get his balance then fell, his head hitting the base of a birch tree. He rolled onto his stomach and started to cry. Then he got on his feet.

"You *suck*, Rory! You *suck!*" He turned and ran into the grove.

Rory opened one of the Coors and took a long drink. He sat on the rock near the garbage barrel and heard Vinnie yell the same words again. The kid had it coming, no doubt about that. And he's lucky too, Rory thought, I could've smacked him but I didn't. I just pushed him.

The tent flap opened and April stuck her head out. One of her braided pigtails had come undone. When she walked toward Rory, he smiled.

"I'm gonna call you half-braid."

She glanced at the beer in his hand. She looked over the food supplies until she found the canteen, then she rinsed out her mouth and drank until she'd swallowed six or seven times. "Did you hit Vinnie?"

"No honey, I didn't hit him. I yelled at him and I pushed him, that's it."

"Why though? We're supposed to be camping."

She sounded like she might start to cry, but when Rory knelt down to hug her she stepped back.

"Where did he go?"

"Just in the woods a little ways. If we keep the fire going good, he'll see us."

Rory pressed his palm to April's forehead. She still felt warm, but she didn't seem as feverish.

"I hate throwing up."

"Feel better?"

She nodded and shivered. Rory took off his jacket and draped it over her shoulders. The leather sleeves covered her hands and hung almost to her knees.

"Want to cook your steak?"

She shook her head.

"Sure?"

"I just want some Coke."

"How 'bout a peanut butter sandwich?"

She shook her head again and looked toward the stream. The fire lit up the rock bed but left the water in darkness. The gurgling rush of it was all Rory could hear.

Without turning her head, April stepped closer to him. "I think I don't like that sound."

"Why hon? It's nice."

"No it's not. It's like it's dying to get away from you for some reason. I like lakes better."

"Strange girl."

"I am *not*."

"Are too."

"Don't *say* that."

"Only kiddin'." Rory sat on the ground against the rock and patted his thighs. April paused then moved to him. She sat on his legs and leaned sideways against his chest. "What if he gets lost?"

"He won't get lost." Rory clasped his hands around her shoulder, but didn't pull her in too close.

"I'm scared."

"No monsters'll getcha while I'm here, sweets."

"Yeah but you're going to jail for a whole year."

"That's true. But you have your mom and brother."

"And Dougie."

"Him too."

April curled in a little closer. "He says you deserve it. He says you should have to stay in jail a long time."

"He says that to you?"

"No, to Vinnie and Mom. Vinnie mostly."

Rory saw himself walking into his old trailer, yanking Cohen off the couch, then tossing him outside where he'd lay into him until nurses couldn't help, just surgeons.

"But I don't listen 'cause I know it was just an accident." She rested her cheek on his shoulder and was quiet. A wood-spark cracked out of the fire onto the dirt. Rory let go of her to sip from his beer. The whiskey flask was pressing against his butt, and he wanted some, but he didn't want to disturb April. He could smell her hair: woodsmoke and little girl sweat, just the hint of cherry shampoo.

"Besides," she said into his shoulder, "I'm not afraid of monsters. I'm just afraid."

"Of what?"

"Everything, Dad. All the time."

RORY FINISHED HIS BEER. He wanted the other but couldn't get to it without moving April. He reached behind him and skinned his knuckles getting the flask out of his back pocket. He unscrewed the cap with his left hand against April's shoulder, then he drank. The Jack was still going down rough. His tongue stiffened against it first, then his throat. When the whiskey reached his stomach, his gut muscles seemed to hold still like they were bracing themselves for bad news. But soon the heat of it down there started to feel good. It'd been three seasons, but his pilot light wasn't out yet. Rory Enfield's furnace was back and cranking up steam. For what? he thought. For everything, God damn it. For April. For the thirteen-year-old boy with his head up his ass in the woods. For the hard-time bullshit Rory knew he might have to face starting Monday. He was glad he hadn't listened to Alene and shaved his beard; he would look more boyish then, he knew.

He sipped from the flask, then lightly rested his chin on the top of April's head. The fire was burning down fast, cracking out sparks that rose up in a heat fume then vanished before the tree-tops. Rory thought of his old man in Derry, the way he'd sit on his back porch with a cold beer at dusk in the summer. His three-quarter-acre lawn would still smell like fresh-cut grass from the day's mowing. The sun'd be going down behind the stand of poplars at the property's edge, and Rory Enfield, Sr., dressed in cutoff jeans and a white V-neck T-shirt, would be sipping a can of Olympia, saying, "Son, if it never gets worse than this, I'm going out happy."

And maybe that's how it felt now. Really. Never mind the particulars, Rory thought. This is a camp we've made for ourselves. This is my ass sitting on the ground in a basin of wild birch trees in the middle of the White Mountains. This is a girl who calls me Daddy. He sipped more Jack. One thing would make this all better, though. No, two. First would be one last ride on the bike. Mick'd been good last night. A true bro' showing true colors. He had taken out his Harley El Glide instead of the Triumph 'cause the Tri's seat was short and flat and Rory would've had to hold on to Mick like a woman. But the El Glide was another story: a cream-colored '69 shovelhead that had a wide Goodyear tire in back and a real narrow one in front off of hydraulic glide forks. It looked like half a chopper with its seat curving up and over the rear tire, so that Rory had sat a head above Mick. And last night, the first time since last July, Rory'd felt the rush of road wind in his face. Like getting baptized with fast air, it was not only part of the thrill, it *was* the thrill. What made a man ride the tar in the first place. And even though it was Mick's sled and not Rory's dream machine—not his Harley 1340 cc Low Rider with the buckhorn handlebars and the red gas tank with *Born to Ride* etched in beneath the HD logo—even though it wasn't that, it would do. And after only one or two Cokes at The Hideaway, then The Eighteenth Wheel, before Mick'd even finished his Miller, Rory had nudged him toward the door to cruise to the next place. And feel free to take the back roads, bro'. Feel free. But Mick had opened it all the way up Amesbury Street and they were still going a C-note when the lights of Aunt Betty's Pub came into view. Mick down-shifted without jarring once and they pulled into the parking lot behind pickup trucks and vans, the little Jap cars of the bank tellers and secretaries who Rory knew got wet over guys like him and Mick. They had a kid or two at home and no man. Pretty spiders in a pretty web. Mick parked his sled and they'd gone inside where Rory drank a Coke and thought about tonight and Jack Daniel's and the kids.

The flask was quickly losing weight. Rory capped it. He'd want some after the steaks, he knew. But you can't cook steaks without a fire and he realized there wasn't much of one left. So where was all this light coming from? He could see the tent clearly. He could even make out the black lines in the birch trunks. It was the moon. Its light was everywhere. The clearing and stream were bathed in it, and where the water foamed over the rocks was no longer white but pale blue. Rory remembered Vinnie, the second thing that'd make this night better, and he pulled gently on April's shoulder. "Honey, let's get up."

She moaned and curled in closer then she raised her head and stood up all at once. She started toward the fire's coals, stopped, and crawled into the tent. Rory's legs were asleep. He drew his right leg up, then his left. He had no idea what time it was, though it seemed late.

"He's not here, Dad. Where is he?"

"He's spyin' on us. You watch, he's gonna ambush us."

"No, really, where is he?"

Rory sat on the rock behind him. As soon as he could feel his toes he stood and walked to the coals and April. "Vinnie! Yo, *Vin!*"

There was no answer, but the stream seemed louder than before.

"I'm cold."

"Me too, listen up. I'm gonna start the fire again, then I'm gonna go get your brother."

"What about me?"

"You'll be okay here, April Smapril. I want you to stay warm."

"You're leaving me alone?"

"How do you figure? Look at all these trees around you. Check out those stars up there. Seems like a good party to me." Rory gathered up scattered bark left over from the woodpile and laid it on the coals. He got down on his hands and knees and blew until there were flames. He rested two of the hickory logs on it, and while they were catching he ducked inside the tent to get April's flashlight. It was still turned on and her vomit was all over it. Rory wiped it clean with his steak-sauce bandana from the corner. Outside, April was standing close to the fire looking up at the black ridge of Crawford Notch against the sky. Rory tucked the light under his chin and pissed into the darkness. "Know why you can see those stars so good?"

April shook her head.

"'Cause there's no fake light down here to mess it up."

"It's like we're on the moon."

"That's right, a friendly moon." Rory shook himself dry, zipped up, then took a hit off the JD flask. "I'll go get Vinnie and be right back. There's candy bars and peanut butter over by the rock. And we'll cook those steaks."

"Dad?" She was looking at him now. In the firelight, with one pigtail loose and the other braided, the motorcycle jacket hanging on her like a leather nightgown, her face took on the shadows of a woman and she looked so much like Alene Rory felt a shiver. But there was more too; she not only looked like her mother, she seemed to reflect that pure part of her that Alene didn't even have anymore.

"Vinnie and Doug don't like each other. Vinnie's always telling Dougie you can beat him up anytime you want. Mom tells him to shut up, that you're bad and Doug's good; but Vinnie wants to be just like you."

Rory didn't know what to say. He hadn't thought of that, not after this past year. He turned and headed into the trees.

First he went in the direction Vinnie had gone. He shined the flashlight on the birches in front of him and was back on the trail in no time. But this wasn't the trail they'd used to get to the camp. That one had ended in the clearing. This one was wide and over-grown with ferns. Rory pointed his flashlight south. Ten or twelve feet down, the trail seemed to spread out and end itself in the grove. North, the fern trail went up a rise and he climbed it. Just before he reached the top he tripped on what felt like a rock. He fell forward on his hands, the flashlight breaking under him. He stood and shook it, heard the broken glass, then threw it as hard as he could into the air. It came down in the trees and he thought how nice it'd be if it hit Vinnie on his crybaby head.

He uncapped the flask and drank. This moonlight was the balls. Even in these trees he could see fifteen, twenty yards all around him. Who needs a flashlight? With the open flask in his hand he walked through the ferns to the top of the rise. He could see the moon. It was low and almost full. It looked like it was sitting on the north ridge leading to Crawford Notch. Humpty Dumpty sat on the wall. Humpty Dumpty had a big fall.

Rory drank again.

The trail dropped steeply, and halfway down, the whiteness of the birches ended and the jack pines began. Rory was going faster than he wanted so he caught hold of a tree trunk to slow himself. He hooked his arm around it and let himself swing back and forth. The air was still, almost icy, and he wondered if there was ever any wind in this basin. He ran his fingers through his beard, then he let go of the tree and ran down the last of the trail.

As soon as he stopped, he saw it. Straight ahead and off to the right, in front of a massive chunk of granite, was a small campfire. Vinnie was sitting beside it with his back to Rory. Rory began to tiptoe through the ferns, but then changed his mind. Fuck this; this was serious shit. *"Hey."*

Vinnie turned around and peered into the dark just as Rory stepped into the firelight and leaned against the boulder. "You've pissed me off today, Vin."

"I don't care."

Rory let out a long breath and followed it with a chug off the flask. Vinnie kept his eyes on the flames. His brown hair hung over his forehead. Because his face was round there were no shadows in it; and he looked younger than thirteen. Man, he was just a baby.

"It's a drag you hit your head."

Vinnie was quiet but Rory saw him swallow.

"You must be starvin', huh? *I* am." Rory walked around the fire, but when he started to sit he lost his balance and had to lean on the boy's shoulder on the way down.

Vinnie twisted away.

Rory laughed. He didn't know why he did, and it sounded as wrong to him as laughing could. Like somebody farting when they're making love. He closed his mouth and put the flask to it. Oops. Not much left. Vinnie might like some. He held it out to him.

The boy picked up a stick beside him and poked at the coals. "Ignorin' me?"

"No."

"You're not? Looks like it to me. Looks like you don't give a *shit* about me anymore, Vin."

"Everybody sucks. I don't care about anybody."

"Smart kid. You're right. Everybody does suck." Rory raised the flask to his lips then lowered it. "Everybody but you and April. You kids are the balls. I'm havin' a great time with you two. There's nobody I'd rather be with tonight. I mean it." Rory upended the flask until it was empty. He dropped it behind his back to the ground. The world was sweet and ugly, yes it was.

"How can you *drink?*"

"Hey buddy, hey palsy, hey pal, don't ask so many big questions. Let me ask one. How the fuck you get this fire goin'?"

Vinnie held the lighter out. Rory didn't take it. He looked at how the fire lit up the silver sculpture of the lone horseman in Vinnie's palm. Then he took the Bic and squeezed it, tried to hold down what was coming, but it had started before he ever realized he was in the danger zone. He hunched his shoulders as he cried. It came out in three spasms. He took a deep breath. The rest he could hold off, he knew. He might be sittin' in the toilet, but he wasn't going to turn to blubber in front of Alene's boy. No way, palsies. Forget that.

Vinnie stood and kicked dirt onto the fire. Rory stood too, but the world became a merry-go-round that smacked his butt, then the back of his head. Things were really whizzing. The night sky. The tops of trees. He sat up and watched Vinnie stomp on the coals with his shitkicker boots. "'Member that flick, Vin? When the witch melted down to nothin'? You look like you're stampin' her out, man. Jesus, Mighty Vincent: Killer of Witches, Son of Bitches."

"Watch it."

"What?"

"What you just said."

"What's wrong with killing witches, man?"

"No, what you said about my mom. Don't you ever say anything about her. Ever."

"Why, Vin? What's she say good about me? *Huh?!* Tell me!"

He got on his hands and knees and when he stood, he stepped on the lighter. He stooped to pick it up then fell forward toward Vinnie. The boy pushed at him and sidestepped out of the way. Rory spun half around. The boulder slapped his back. He leaned against it, then took a step and threw the lighter as hard as he could into the trees. *"I never even cheated!"*

He shook his head. "Man, I don't deserve this. No way in hell do I deserve this. She let me down. She really did."

Vinnie was standing still. "April's alone. We should go."

"*She's* alone. Shit, she's got Dougie. No sweetheart's visitin' me in that Gray Bar Motel. Forget it, bud."

"I said April."

In the moonlight Rory couldn't read Vinnie's face, but the kid was standing sideways like he was getting ready to walk up the trail and leave Rory where he stood. Like Rory Enfield was a pitiful piece of shit that deserved what he was getting. He remem-

bered what the boy had said on the rock overlooking Crawford
Notch, about somebody knowing what heaven looks like and it
ain't God. Rory knew he should spank this kid right now, just put
him over his knee 'til he knows the deal. Then a thought came to
him that was like ice cream in his stomach: maybe Vinnie didn't
know. Maybe Alene'd lied to him about the facts. Maybe the kid
was confused.

"Hey. I know last-summer talk is taboo, but you know the guy
had cancer, right? He was sixty-three years old and his asshole
was sewn shut 'cause a the cancer. That's why he wasn't wearing a
seat belt. 'Cause it pressed against his shit bag. You know this,
right?"

Vinnie didn't move.

"I mean, that's one thing I feel okay about. Really. I think in
some way I helped that friggin' guy. I did."

Vinnie was walking back up the trail toward camp. Rory
couldn't remember seeing him turn and head off. He pushed himself away from the boulder. If he could just hold the kid's shoulders and look him in the face, if he could just do that, just hold the
kid still, then he'd understand, he'd know that Rory Enfield was a
man eatin' a lot of shit these days for no reason, a guy who
worked hard and paid his bills.

"I'm clean, man. I got nothin' to be ashamed of. *Nothin'*."

Rory was halfway up the hill between the trees, but he wasn't
moving. He couldn't remember getting here. The moonshine was
everywhere and he didn't like it anymore; it made him feel like he
was at the bottom of the ocean black. He tried hard to make it up
the hill but things weren't working. He was clutching fern roots in
his hands and he knew if he let go of them that he'd be pulled
away by the current of the world. Night was spinning again, but

in his head things were well lit and still: he could see her face, smoking a Merit, telling him she's in love with this nurse named Doug and this guy Doug is what I really need in a man. Not you, Rory. Not you. You turn over the kitchen table so you don't smack her. Then it's open-throttle time down to The Hideaway where you meet Mick Welch. It's having to go talk by the jukebox because the bar is full and you feel like you might start gushing. It's leaving there and gunning your Low Rider past Mick's El Glide like nothin'. It's pulling into Aunt Betty's Pub and coming on to Carol Jean because her old man Slim Jim is there and you're hoping he'll say something. It's drinking five shots of JD in a half hour and walking out of the bar when Mick's still in the head. It's El Speedo time up Whittier Hill, your headlight lighting up the trees as you whiz by, your head full of her face, her dry eyes, her blond hair. It's downshifting from seventy to twenty-five 'cause all of a sudden you want to see the moon on the ocean at Salisbury Beach. You turn off onto the northbound ramp to the highway, then pedal-shift into higher gear under a starlit sky, which you look up at now because, fuck it; stars never lie. Sailors lived by 'em for years. But you're not quite off the ramp yet and while you're still looking for the Little Dipper, your front wheel whacks the median strip, your buckhorn handlebars yank sharp to the left and you're holding on to nothing but air. Then it's the smack of the road against your shoulder and hip and you're rolling across the highway. Your Low Rider has jumped the strip and is sliding along beside you, sparking its way to the fast lane where it comes to a stop, but you don't. You roll right onto soft grass then down a short but steep hill that leaves you lying in a slimy concrete culvert. You're flat on your back and you don't see anything fixed. Everything's whipping in a circle so you close your eyes, but then it's worse. You open them and feel the gutter-wash push past your leather jacket collar down your back. You're hoping none of this juice is coming from you, but you don't really care.

Then you *do* care.

You don't want to go to the beach anymore. You want to go back to the trailer where you'll pick up the table if she hasn't already. Where you'll brew some coffee, take a shower, then talk low and gently to your wife. No. You'll listen. Fools talk, wise dudes listen. Because you want to know. You want to understand the blueprints of her thinking. You want to feel the pulls and pushes of her heart. Then you want to get inside it and push when she does, pull when she does, but a tad more, 'til she thinks you are her and she is you and separated neither one of you will make it. It might take days. Weeks. But she owes you that, right? This is Alene.

So you lay your arms over your chest. Good, movement. You cross your ankles and you know your legs still work. No real damage. And just as the word *damage* passes through your brain, your stomach muscles twist up and you turn on your side so your puke doesn't bubble out over your face. It's all sour mash, and it's over fast.

You start to crawl back up the hill. Your body feels heavy and you're breathing hard. Your head is clear, though. You feel all right. You're a lucky bastard and you know it. Everything about this stings like a second chance. You have to rest, so you roll onto your back and slide down the hill about three inches. On the other side of the culvert, over the southbound lanes, there is a streetlight flickering, but here it's dark. Even with the stars, it's dark. And quiet. You actually start to think about the weather tomorrow and how good it will be framing in the sun. It's time to go home, though, to make sure you still got one. A car goes by southbound. Then you hear one coming up the pike. Good, you think. I'll need a ride. You turn and start back up the hill, clutching clumps of grass and pushing off with the sides of your boots. You're almost there when something changes: sound. The sure and steady roll of a car moving along the way it should turns to this: you hear the lock of wheel brakes. Then, like the tires themselves are terrified, you hear the long whine of rubber burning its way to what the car's trying to avoid. Then it comes—like all that stopping did nothing—the thunderous clap of steel on steel, the scrape and clattering thunk of your Low Rider getting run over then dragged.

Everything is quiet. You make it up the hill to see a late-model Dodge Dart sitting on your bike, but the headlights are off and they're facing you when they should be facing north. You don't move. The car's windshield is shattered. You can't see how many people are inside.

All you hear is the trickle of oil or gas coming out of the car, or your bike, or both.

RORY JERKED AND WOKE UP. Above him, the high leaves of paper birches flittered in a breeze he didn't feel. The sky was cloudless and had the deep blue you see when you're up there in a plane. He heard the flowing water behind him, then the shrill cry of a bird he couldn't name, and as soon as he heard that he knew he'd been drunk, probably still was, and that bird was shrieking it out to everyone. When he sat up, his sleeping bag fell away from him. His leather jacket was folded up on the ground where his head had been. He imagined little April taking it off and making a pillow for him. How did he get here? Vinnie? Both of them?

There was no fire left at all, just fine ash. He stood. The air was cool, almost cold. He looked east behind the tent through the trees, but couldn't see the sun yet. It was probably six, six-thirty. The tent flap was down. He wondered about April's fever, her flu. He started to run his fingers through his beard, but stopped when he felt the dried stickiness of it. He looked down at his boots. There wasn't anything on them or on his pants, but his black Hideaway Lounge T-shirt was damp and stiff with puke. That meant he'd done it lying down. He could've suffocated out here in the mountains and left those two beauties to fend for themselves. He'd been clean all these months, on the straight and narrow, and not just because they took a piss sample down at the station, not that. And it wasn't the Wednesday night meetings either, it was me, Rory thought. *I* liked it. I was working better, and feeling better. Even looking good again. Lost some gut. Got all the whites of my eyes back. And I swore I'd never blow blood again. Never.

He turned, yanked off his T-shirt, and walked to the stream. He pissed on a scrub pine at the water's edge, then he lay down on his belly and drank until his gut felt tight. He untied his boots, kicked them off, and got out of his jeans and underpants. He stepped into the water and Sweet Jesus, oh Lord it was colder than last night. He put both feet in and heard the cry of the bird behind and above him. But this time its sound seemed okay. It was saying, "Go on, Rore. Cleanse thyself. We're all behind ya, kid."

Rory waded in to his knees. His balls shrunk and curled up into their sac. He took a deep breath and looked up at Crawford Notch. On the northern slope were two short cliffs of granite. The sun was catching them and they were almost too bright to look straight at, but they were glorious. No guts, no glory, Rory. He didn't know if he'd just said that or thought it. It didn't matter. He sat down cross-legged in the stream. The water was so cold it seemed to push through his flesh to his bones where it was working on breaking them. He let out three quick breaths, held it, then leaned over sideways against the current until his head and face and whole body were in it. He scrubbed his beard and kept his eyes shut. Then he opened them, and through the hazy water, he saw a twig wedged between two white rocks. But it wasn't a twig at all; it was a black wooden cross looking right at him. Rory sat up fast and shook the water out of his hair. Every bit of him wanted to high-step it out of the stream back to his clothes, but instead, he rose slowly and walked. He squatted, rinsed his T-shirt off in the stream, then wrung it out on a flat rock in the sun. He pulled on his underwear and jeans, rolled the cuffs up to mid-shin, then glanced at the tent before he went back over the rocks in the stream to the field on the other side. He gathered broken twigs and thin branches from around the trunk of the fallen hickory. When he had an armful, he carried it back to the camp and set it quietly on the ashes. At the food pile, he picked up the three wrapped steaks. They were soft now, but they still felt cold. He laid them neatly on the pack that was still draped over the garbage barrel.

Back in the field, he hoped the kids wouldn't wake up until he had breakfast ready. Steak, oatmeal, toast and coffee. Did they drink coffee? The branches were too thick now for him to break at their base without his boots, but with his hands, Rory was able to twist off the tips of some. It was taking a long time and he was beginning to sweat. Then came the thirst again. The Jack Daniel's Desert. And he had to go to the stream three times before he was finished. When he finally stepped over the rocks, carrying the wood in front of him with both arms, he could see the sun above the trees of the basin. He felt good, almost giddy. He laid the wood down then went back to the stream and pulled on his boots, leaving them unlaced. His T-shirt was still damp so he put on his motorcycle jacket. Truth is, though, he wanted to stay naked. That'd felt good. So new. But what if April crawled out of her sleep and saw him bare-assed? That wasn't right.

He ate a candy bar. There were only two left and the marshmallows were gone. That was bad, he thought. Got to cook those steaks. Rory spread candy bar wrappers over the fire's ashes, then laid the kindling on top. He patted his jeans pocket for his lighter. He remembered giving it to Vinnie last night. He didn't want to wake the kid up, but he didn't want them coming out of the tent until he had breakfast ready either. He wanted them to open their eyes and noses, their very lives, to the smells of steaming oatmeal and cooking meat, hot coffee. Maybe he could go through Vinnie's pockets without waking him up. Rory was just about to go inside the tent when he heard low voices, then saw Vinnie stick his head out the flap. His hair was messed up and he was squinting first at the stream, then at Rory. "Hi."

"Mornin', partner. How 'bout tossing my lighter so I can feed us."

Vinnie looked up at Rory like he'd just been told he was pregnant with a salamander. "Don't you remember? You whipped it into the woods."

"When did I whip it into the woods?"

"When else?" Vinnie walked past the garbage barrel and peed. He had his wool sweater and jeans on, but was barefoot.

"Dad?" April came out of the tent. She was wearing her sneakers, jeans, and a yellow sweater with pink and blue roses on the shoulders. Her hair was hanging loose, no more braids. She looked older. "I still don't feel good."

"You will after we eat, hon'. Look at this *day*."

April walked around behind the tent. Vinnie was sitting on the rock eating an Almond Joy bar, looking at Rory while he chewed.

"What?"

"Nothin'."

Rory turned to build the fire again. He remembered what Vinnie'd said about the lighter. He looked at the boy looking at him. The kid had to be right, no doubt about that. Everything in his face said so, said: You're a fuck-up, Rory, and how you ever got me and my sister out on this camping trip, I'll never know. You're bad news nobody wants to hear, mister. So can we go home now or what?

"What about these steaks?"

Vinnie shrugged.

"They cost money, you know."

"Don't look at me. I didn't do nothin'."

Vinnie's voice sounded high. Rory could hear the hurt in it. April walked back around from behind the tent.

"Wish we had some toilet paper. We should have brought some."

"*Hey,* I'm sorry, all *right?* Do I have to do everything on this goddamned—" Rory stopped himself. It was the instant surprise in April's face. She'd been looking at Vinnie when she said it. She wasn't blaming anybody for anything. In fact, she looked like she was scolding herself. Now she looked like she might cry.

"I'm sorry, sweets. I don't mean to yell. God, I don't mean to do anything bad. I just wanted to make us a hot breakfast and now I can't 'cause a my own foolishness."

"Yeah," Vinnie said, "but you were sad 'cause Mom gave you that and now you're going to jail 'cause she cheated on you."

Rory wanted to answer right away but felt he might gush some if he did. April sat on the ground, opened the peanut butter, and stuck her finger inside.

"Thanks, Vin. I appreciate what you're saying. It means a lot to me. It does. But I'm not going to prison because of your mom. I'm going because of me."

April opened the bread, took out six slices, and started to make sandwiches. Vinnie leaned back against the tree, his eyes on Rory's.

"See, a judge makes me go to these meetings every Wednesday night."

"We know. AA."

"Alcoholics Amonymous."

"Right, amonymous. Anyway, these people have a sayin' for what I did last night. They call it a slip. But I want you two to know somethin'. I didn't slip, I planned to drink last night. I won't see you kids for a long time, or if I do, it'll be in a shitty little visiting room. And I haven't had a drop since last summer. Almost a whole year. So I gave myself a treat."

"Like when you and Mom used to take us to Friendly's for chocolate banana boats?" April held a peanut butter sandwich out to him.

"Yeah, like that." Rory took it. He started to take a bite, but its oily nut smell made him feel queasy. Vinnie was halfway through his when he said with a full mouth: "Doug doesn't drink at all."

"What's that, Vin? I didn't hear."

Vinnie swallowed and took another bite. "I said, Doug never drinks."

"*Jesus,* one more word about that asshole from you and I swear to Christ I'm gonna smack ya right here."

What was happening now seemed to Rory dreamlike, not real,

not going on at all. Vinnie threw his sandwich down and ran into the tent. Rory heard first one sleeping bag being zipped, then the other. He cocked his head to the side so that he could hear better. April was quiet and Rory did not look down at her.

Vinnie came out of the tent on his knees. He had a rolled sleeping bag beneath each arm. His pack was strapped onto him and he had put on his shoes.

"What's up?" Rory felt nothing as he said it. The words seemed to come out of him only like something he almost forgot to say. He was breathing real easy, and for a second he saw himself taking a naked nap in the sun.

Vinnie bent over and grabbed April's arm. "Come on, we're thumbin' home."

April jerked away and stood up fast. She looked from her brother to Rory.

Rory stared back. Her face was pale and completely unmoving. Her lips were parted somewhere between confusion and disbelief. What did she want him to do? Tie Vinnie to a tree? She kept her eyes on Rory and he said nothing. There was nothing to say. Nothing to do. Nothing. You do what you can, then you die. Period.

"Come on, April. I'm goin'."

Vinnie's words were the rock in the still lake of her face. She was crying. Loud and all at once. Red face. Wet cheeks. Snot in her nose, her eyes still on Rory. He watched her for a second, maybe two, then, whatever had been just not-happening was happening now, was real, and was real goddamned serious. He stepped toward her to hug her, but she backed away shaking her head and crying even louder, looking from Rory to Vinnie and back again. "I hate it. You're so stupid. You're both so *stupid*."

She turned and ran up the trail, her blond hair bouncing, the green soles of her pink sneakers showing themselves, then hitting the ground, then showing themselves. Vinnie was walking after her with a sleeping bag beneath each arm, looking straight ahead, his pack secure, his head up.

Well that's that, Rory thought. That's fucking that. Beautiful. Wonderful. A great weekend was had by all. G'bye, Daddy. We love you. We'll miss you. Hope you don't get too lonesome in jail. Hope nobody tries to hurt you in there. We'll write you letters every day and send you pictures we draw and homework we get A's on and cookies, if you want. There's nobody like you, Daddy, nobody in the whole world. Really.

Rory started for the stream, stopped, started for the tent, stopped. He sat on the rock near the garbage barrel and leaned back against the tree. He glanced down at the open Wonder Bread loaf and the peanut butter jar, the oatmeal box, the instant coffee, the full mustard jar and brick of cheese, April's untouched sandwich. Vinnie's strapless canteen. A seven-mile hike under the sun without water. Wonderful. Good work, Rory. Cohen gives him a new canteen and you carve it up. Alene gives you something that should've lasted forever, and you whip it into the woods. Little April makes you a sandwich and you don't eat it. There was something else with her too. Then he remembered her flashlight, throwing it out over the birches wishing for it to land on Vinnie's head. Nice. Real nice. And there was that too; the boy must have a bump on the back of his head the size of a plumb bob. Rory looked across the clearing at the tree Vinnie'd fallen against. He remembered how young and pudgy, how so scared the boy had looked as he flailed his arms on the way down and got hurt anyway.

Rory squeezed his eyes shut. He held his breath too. His heart had picked up the tempo in its fast but uneven hungover dance, like it wanted to get the day over with because it was both ashamed and weakened by the quality of blood it was given to pump out to the rest of the body. Rory opened his eyes and saw the other Coors on the ground next to the aluminum pot. He picked up the beer, opened it, and took a long drink. It wasn't cold, it was cool, and Rory thought it'd be better if it was hot. A hot beer. That would be better punishment. 'Cause that is what I'm doing, he thought. I am punishing myself. Cleanse thyself with poison, somebody said. Who was it? Rory couldn't remember. It didn't matter. None of these bullshit slogans mattered: One Day at a Time, Live and Let Live, Easy Does It, Let Go and Let God. Well, maybe there was something to that one, he thought. Maybe the Big Guy knows when to put you in the slammer before it's too late. Rory smiled at this picture in his head of God, looking like Jesus but fatter, with long robes and a beard, his hands cupped to his mouth shouting down to earth, "Hey Enfield! Last call for alcohol! You don't have to go home but you *can't stay here.*"

And he's right too, Rory thought as he finished the Coors and tossed it in the direction of the garbage barrel, watched it bounce off the wrapped steaks and hit the ground. I can't stay here and I'm not gonna let Vinnie and April walk seven miles without cold water either. Forget that one. It won't happen. Rory Enfield, Jr., may be a lush, but he's not a ratbastard. And he doesn't litter either. He picked up the can and dropped it into the barrel. He set the steaks on the ground, carried his empty pack to the food pile, squatted, and put the jar of instant coffee inside, then he stopped and took it out. What am I doing? he thought. This shit'll weigh a ton; it's going in the garbage. Then came another voice: Garbage?

This ain't garbage. Mick and Marie drink instant. They like cheese too. And mustard. They won't touch the oatmeal, but give it to Alene and the kids. And Doug. Yes, him too. Try leaving a trail of goodness, Rory. See what that's like. And be grateful, man. Yes, he thought. I've got to make up a gratitude list right now. He sat back against his calves and closed his eyes. I thank my Higher Power for the following:

I can walk.

I can talk.

My dick still gets hard.

I can work.

I can still see the kids.

I have good friends.

I could have gotten five years, but I only got two and will only do one.

And thank you, oh thank you, there were no kids in the car.

And no women.

No teenage lovers.

Just an old guy who must have seen my bike, must have. Who didn't want to miss it really. Who wanted it to be over fast before it was over slow.

Thank you, God. Thanks for everything.

I won't let you down.

When he finished loading the food and aluminum pot into the pack, Rory took the canteen to the stream and dipped it in. He watched the air bubbling out of it as it filled. The water felt colder than ever but the air was warmer and the sky was cloudless. When the canteen was full Rory pulled off his belt. His Puma fell to the rocks but he ignored it and worked the leather through the two metal rings, then secured the buckle and hung the canteen over his leather-jacketed shoulder and across his bare chest. He pulled the knife from its sheath, walked to the tent, and cut the canteen strap from where it held the five tent poles together at the top. He burped twice as he rolled up the canvas and aluminum poles, as he tied them into the top section of the pack's frame.

He knew he had to hurry. He had seen how fast those kids could move over the trail like fine young mountain animals. They were gonna be real thirsty. Especially April, with her leftover flu. Rory zipped his jacket up three or four inches so the leather wouldn't flap against his belly on the walk. He squatted in front of the pack and worked his right arm through the strap, then his left. When he stood the frame pushed against the canteen which pinched his skin at the waist. He arched his back and moved his shoulders until the weight of everything settled in the way it was going to. He looked the camp over once to make sure it was like they'd found it. Except for the ashes and the matted spot where they'd set up the tent, everything looked fine. There was a breeze going now, and the green buds of the birches wavered in it. He turned and started for the trail when white caught his eye from the ground. Trash. Nope, the steaks. Damn. He didn't want to take the time to pack them; there was no time to take. April could get seriously sick today walking hard without water and that's not the legacy I'm leaving behind, he thought. Forget it. He knelt, almost fell forward, grabbed the steaks and dropped them into the barrel.

He was thirsty again. The beer had made it worse, but as he headed into the shade of the birch trail, the pack's straps pulling into his shoulders and the full canteen knocking against his hip, he told himself he wouldn't touch a drop until the kids drank first. Not one.

The air was cooler here and he lengthened his stride. His belt was rubbing against his bare chest and he remembered his T-shirt and Puma knife sheath still by the stream. He glanced to his right through the stand of birch trees, but could only see some scattered spruce at the base of Crawford Notch on the other side. He could still hear the water though. And as he moved farther away from it, listening to its steady gush, Rory wished he'd unwrapped the steaks and tossed them into the current. All three had felt soft and warm. Tomorrow, they would start to stink.

LAST DANCE

In Memory of Elmer Lamar Lowe

Reilly stuck his arm out the truck window and let the hot wind catch in his palm and push at his arm. He looked out at the thin pines and cracked red clay moving by, listened to Billy Wayne humming along with the radio; he thought of how bad Billy looked, saw the waxy yellow look of his skin, the gray under his eyes, tried to imagine him down in the parish jail near Leesville with nothing to drink and nobody to mess with.

"How 'bout another 'Staff, Cap?" Billy Wayne said from behind the wheel.

Reilly reached into the brown paper bag and pulled another Falstaff out, handed it to Billy Wayne.

"Thank you, Cap."

Merle Haggard came on the radio, his voice sad and whiskey deep. Billy turned him up and looked over at Reilly.

"Son, that man can *sing*."

"What happened to your teeth, BW?"

Billy Wayne scrunched up his face like somebody had just pinched him. "Jude, that bitch."

Reilly remembered her: dark hair and eyes, her fierce little body chain-smoking Raleighs, making coffee in Billy Wayne's kitchen, in the old house he won in a game of draw down at Le Mae's. She was as old as his mother but he felt something happen whenever she looked his way, when she would smile at one of his jokes about Billy Wayne.

"Cap, what you're lookin' at is the by-product of a hot iron skillet full of corn bread. The bitch even suckered me with it."

"Jesus."

Billy turned to Reilly and pulled his upper lip to his nose. "See for yourself."

Reilly looked at his yellow-pink gums, saw that some of the parts looked full with the roots of the teeth still in them, others were sagging and empty where the teeth had been completely torn out, and there was one place in the middle that still had a jagged piece of tooth hanging out of the gum, a broken gray stalactite in Billy Wayne's mouth. "Shit," Reilly said.

Billy Wayne turned his head back to the road and drank from his beer.

They turned off I-65 just past Mister Ed's barbecue and drove down a narrow two-lane road with no center dividing line.

Reilly drained his beer and popped open another.

"How much daylight you figure we got left?"

"Couple hours."

"You check it this morning?"

"Son, I've checked that net three times today."

Reilly watched Billy Wayne finish his beer in one quick drop and rise of his Adam's apple then toss the can out the window.

"And I'll tell ya somethin' right now, Cap, we're gonna get her tonight, I can feel it." Billy Wayne put his hand out to Reilly, his eyes still on the road.

"We're out."

Billy looked over at him, his eyes opening wide with the panic Reilly could feel, like he'd just been told to swim the width of Dry Patch Lake underwater. "Then you're going to have to share that one with me 'til we get to Red Willie's."

Reilly shuddered with the thought. "Here," he said, "you can finish it."

Red Willie's place sat on a small hill by the river, an unpainted one-room shack with wide cracks between its weathered boards, with knotholes rotten all the way through, so that at night the naked light bulb Red drank to lit up the outside as well, shone on the beer cans and rusted metal of his dirt yard. Reilly knew Billy hadn't seen Red since he got out, and as the truck swayed with the ruts in the road, he hoped Red was home.

Billy Wayne turned off the radio and they drove the last quarter mile in silence. The road was made of gravel and was so narrow that the driver of an oncoming car or truck had to pull over against the bush and trees to let the other by. Reilly reached his hand out at a thin branch, thought of growing up in Ayer's Village, Massachusetts, where you put your life in somebody else's hands at intersections ("They've all got a death wish," his stepfather had said). Where people's faces looked stony and blanched from working inside factories, smoking a lot of cigarettes, and eating too much food out of a can. People who would never stop first on this kind of road, Reilly thought, would keep a tire iron under their seat if they had to drive along it at all.

The road dipped down and moved closer to the river. Billy Wayne slowed the truck just before the turn that would bring them to Red's place and sat up straight, ran his red-splotched hand through the rough of his flattop. Reilly smiled at Billy's shyness, looked over at this man twice his age who talked to Reilly like he'd known him twenty years instead of three summers, who called him Cap for Captain (who had told Reilly once, "Before you think on anything else serious in life, Cap, get yourself a *good woman*"), who had just been left toothless by pretty Jude, who never talked about his rich brother in Texas or his father who Reilly knew had died on a barstool in New Orleans, and who openly declared himself the second best loggerhead turtle catcher in Grant Parish. ("Hell, that old man, he can feel them turtles move a mile away, Cap," Billy had said. "That Red Willie, why shit, *he's* the king.")

Reilly looked out the window through the trees and saw the sparkle of the sun on the river, Red's shack. Billy Wayne pulled the truck into Red's yard, stopped short of running over a rusted set of bedsprings. He turned off the motor and they got out, walked around the side of the shack to the back porch, a small rickety structure that faced the river. Reilly hadn't seen Red since he dropped off that crankshaft from his grandfather's tractor last August, before he had taken a Greyhound back east, and now, looking over the dirt hill Red lived on, Reilly could hardly believe his eyes; empty Falstaff and Budweiser cans, that's all there was, scattered from the porch right down the hill to the trees hanging over the river, Reilly couldn't see the ground. "Billy Wayne," Reilly whispered. "He do all this by himself?"

"I b'lieve your gran'daddy has hepped him now and again." Billy Wayne winked at Reilly as they shuffled and kicked their way through them to the porch.

"What in the *hell?*"

Reilly stepped back as the old man's Winchester poked through the tattered mosquito netting hanging over the door.

"Whoa there now, Mr. Red, we's family now!" Billy Wayne shouted, his hands over his head.

The old man came out from behind the netting, stuck the barrel snug up against Billy's Adam's apple. "One of these days, William, I'm going to give you a second mouth."

Billy didn't say anything. Reilly tried to force a laugh, but it got caught in his throat. He looked at the old man's eyes, glassy blue and set deep in his face. He wasn't wearing a shirt or shoes and his faded overalls were held up over one shoulder by a rusty diaper pin with a broken pink clasp.

Billy Wayne let out a nervous laugh that started somewhere in his nose. Then Red snapped his rifle back quick, set it against the wall.

"You ornry old sonuvabitch."

"Convict."

"Fuck you, Red."

Reilly could hear the hurt in Billy Wayne's voice.

"Now"—Red put his hand on Billy's shoulder—"correct me if I'm wrong, Billy Wayne, but word has it you done time for sellin' your own wife's rented furniture. That right?"

Reilly looked at how straight Billy was standing, thought of Billy's father, the last minutes of his life spent looking at the world cross-eyed, his stomach queasy, chest tight.

"It was ugly shit, Red."

The old man's face exploded with laughter; he slapped Billy Wayne hard on the shoulder, bent over, and held his stomach with one hand. "Hoowee! Ole BW has returned!"

"You ain't just a woofin' it there, boy," Billy Wayne said, laughing with him.

Red straightened up, looked over at Reilly, still laughing, his eyes shiny. "Hey yank."

"How're you, Red?"

Red Willie nodded then looked back at Billy Wayne. "What're y'all drinkin' this evenin'."

"Whatever in the hell you got."

The old man turned and went back through the netting into the shack. "I got Bud, Bud, and Bud."

REILLY SAT WITH HIS BACK against the cab of the truck, his legs stretched out in front of him. He drank from his beer and looked straight ahead at the narrow gray asphalt moving away from him, rolling out from under the truck like a hard carpet Billy Wayne's Ford was laying. He let his head roll back against the glass and heard Billy Wayne inside, the loud wet-mouthed chatter that came from him whenever he was drunk around Red Willie, drunk and thinking about loggerhead turtles.

"I'll tell ya somethin', Red, you coulda saddled up that damn loggerhead and used her to get groceries. That bitch weighed close to ninety pounds on my scale. I ain't a shittin' ya either."

Reilly couldn't hear Red's response. He looked up at the narrow strip of sky between the moving pine tops, saw the pale blue and gray, the sun's colors gone, and he imagined them wading through the muddy creek with flashlights; he would point his at the place under the trees where the water had moved away the sand, had left bare roots for cottonmouths to rest behind, small wood- and dirt-lined caves that Reilly had had nightmares about when he was a boy.

He drained his beer and got another out of Red's burlap sack; they were still cold, sweating in the bag, and as he opened one he took a deep breath and was suddenly aware of the electric beer current running through his head, felt its gentle liquid massage working on his brain, making the rough parts smooth so that the truck's motion, the fast backward movement of the darkening woods, the side-to-side roll of Red's eight-foot gaff, the way the beer foamed down cold over Reilly's knuckles were all things seen from a softer place, a place Reilly had been in all summer with Billy Wayne.

Red Willie put his hand out the window and yelled to Reilly to pass him two more beers. Reilly did, then stood up facing the cab and held on to its roof, let the wind blow against his face. They turned off onto a gravel road and Reilly held on tighter. He thought of Mimi, pictured her standing on the side of the road ahead of him, alone, watching the truck as it sped by, not knowing it was him until it was too late, until he was past her already, his hair blown back away from his sunburned face, holding on to the roof of the car with one hand, an open beer in the other; he wouldn't even look at her, would just leave her in the sprayed gravel behind him, leave her watching what wasn't hers anymore disappear around a curve in the road.

Reilly ducked a pine branch as it came at him and remembered the six or seven other turtle hunts he had been on with Billy Wayne, remembered all of his talk of close to hundred-pound turtles, sixty-five, seventy years old with a beak that could break a broomstick in half, put a nasty hole in your leg, the kind of turtle a man could live on for a couple of months, Billy had said. Billy Wayne had shown him what to look for, to find the deepest part of the creek first, to look for air bubbles "because more 'n likely them sonsabitches lead straight down to a hunerd pounder holdin' her breath in the mud." He had shown Reilly how to string the net line across the creek, to wade across the shallow part then tie it, leaving it just barely touching the water's surface with a baseball-sized cork hooked in at the middle, being pulled by the creek's current two or three inches but no more. They would finish setting it then drink, and sometimes, if it was dark, Billy Wayne would build a fire to keep the mosquitoes away, something to look into.

Last summer Jude had come along once too. Reilly had liked watching Billy Wayne around her then, liked how he didn't spit or fart or kneel at the creek's edge and say, "C'mon you big ugly motherfucker, walk into that net." He called her Sugar Baby and held her hand when she got close to the water, had said "There's been snakes lately, hon." Reilly had laughed when Jude jumped into Billy Wayne and said, "Oh, Billy!," had almost knocked them both into the water. She had brought pot roast sandwiches and a thermos of hot coffee, had set a cloth on the hood of the truck and laid everything out. Billy Wayne and Reilly built a fire and they had eaten around it, had looked into it and listened to the crackling sound of burning wood, Billy's smacking. After, Billy had poured Jim Beam into his coffee and walked down to the creek while Reilly helped Jude clean up. She was wearing khaki shorts and had one of Billy Wayne's shirts tied in a knot at her waist. Reilly had held the bag open for her while she tossed in the paper plates, dirty napkins, and meat-greased aluminum foil.

"This sure is a big deal for him, isn't it Reilly?"

"Seems to be, ma'am," he had said, noticing her legs, pale and thin, and he had looked right between them at the tight khaki crease in the middle and thought of how hot he had heard cool women are supposed to get.

They had dropped him off at his grandparents' near midnight, his pants wet to the crotch, a five-pound snapper in his bag. Billy Wayne's eyes were misted over with the bourbon when he said goodnight and he had swallowed all his burps on the way home, had talked careful and slow around Jude.

Billy Wayne slowed down then pulled off the gravel and parked in a small clearing under the trees. Reilly jumped out fast and was relieving himself at the foot of a tall pine when Red Willie and Billy Wayne got out of the truck.

"Boy Scout my ass," Red Willie said. "How would you like that for supper, yank?"

"Maybe it'll get drunk off it," Reilly said. He zipped up his pants and belched.

"I knew an ole boy down in the jail who drank his own piss," Billy Wayne said, grabbing the sack of beers and Red Willie's gaff out of the truck.

"That makes me want to spit," Reilly said. "Why'd he do that?"

"Wanted to prove a point."

"And what was that, stud?"

"That there ain't *nothin'* as bad as it seems." Billy Wayne paused for effect, his eyes wide open.

"Bullshit," Red said. "Let's kill us a turtle."

Reilly took the gaff from Billy Wayne as Red Willie led the way down the trail. Its heaviness surprised him. He looked closer and saw it was an old eight-foot two-by-four with the edges planed off, a rusty porch-swing hook screwed tight into one end. He imagined Red sitting on his porch overlooking the river, his cheeks sunken, wood shavings all around his feet, working away with the two-handled blade, making a tool to kill food with.

The woods were dark. Red flicked on his flashlight and shined it ahead of him.

"What's your test weight, BW?"

"One hunerd and fifty pounds!"

Reilly laughed. "You ever really catch anything over five pounds, Billy Wayne?"

"Shit, you hear that, Red? I'll tell ya somethin' now, son, and I'll tell ya true. There's turtles in that water hole that you can't even lift, by God!"

Reilly stumbled on the trail then used the gaff to get his balance back. "I've heard that before."

"Red, hey Red, tell this yankee son of a gun about them old turtles we killed."

"Which way's your trap?"

"I got it at the west fork, Red. Go on, Red, tell the kid here about how long it takes them sonsabitches to really die."

Reilly looked in front of him at Billy Wayne's back and heard the tapping of the beer cans in the sack over his shoulder, listened to Billy's heavy breathing over the flat trail.

"Hey yank!" Red called over his shoulder.

"Yeah."

"You think I pull five-pound turtles with that thing you're carryin'? Do you?"

"I wouldn't think so, Red."

"There you go, yank, there you go."

"Hear that, Cap? Cut through that thicket, Red, it's quicker."

They moved through briar bush that pulled against their legs and snapped under their feet. Reilly stepped high to keep from tripping and held the gaff in front of him with two hands. He liked the heavy balanced feel of it, something solid, a good thing to carry in night woods with a weight to bludgeon with and a hook to gouge. He took a deep breath and filled his chest with air, smelled the pine and dry brush, the wood rot of the creek; things were feeling different this time, more like a job to do, and he knew it was because of Red Willie.

They came out onto the trail again and it widened into a pine-needle-covered clearing near the creek. Reilly heard Billy Wayne cough then spit onto the ground. "Let's have the light, Red, I'll show ya."

Reilly followed them down a short embankment to a small sandbar at the creek's edge. His foot sank in and he pulled it out fast, steadied himself with the gaff. Billy Wayne shined the light out over the slow swirling surface of the water at the cork; it was half submerged in the creek, the water flowing over and around it. "That sonuvabitch is pulled back a foot or two."

"Let's have the light," Red said. He followed the length of the line from the cork over the bank to the tree trunk it was tied to, then he brought the light back down again and followed the line on the other side.

"Ooo Jesus, look how tight them sonsabitches are!"

"Where's your bottom rope, Billy?"

"Right behind us."

Red pointed the light at Reilly then behind him at the ground to a coil of nylon rope in the sand, one end leading then disappearing into the water. "Well son, you might see what that hook's for right now." Red handed the flashlight to Billy Wayne.

Reilly stepped out of the way as Red walked over and picked up the coil of rope then started up the embankment with it, dropping some slack behind him as he moved.

"I've been usin' this little hickory here for my pulley, Red."

"Let's have the kid gaff her, Billy."

Reilly heard the wink in Red Willie's voice.

"You and me will do the pullin' from over here." Red threw the length of rope over a bare branch four or five feet above his head. Billy Wayne caught it.

"Now Cap," Billy shouted to Reilly, "soon as we get the net up even with the water I'll jump down there and give ya some light."

"Yep. Okay." Reilly had a sudden need to urinate and as he walked over the sand and stepped into the warm water, his legs felt too springy, his arms and hands too small.

"Get ready, yank! We're about to snag her!"

Reilly spaced his feet apart in the water, one sinking ahead of him in the creek's bottom, the other just barely in it behind him. He held the gaff well in front of him then turned it around once in his hands so that the hook's point was facing down.

"Pull!"

Reilly took a deep breath and heard the whine of the rope over the branch, Red's grunting, Billy Wayne's breathing. The water dripped off it, moving high and to his right; he narrowed his eyes and could not see the current on the water's surface but felt it against his feet and ankles, could hear it flowing over and around the cork out there ahead of him. He gripped the gaff tighter and thought of black snakes slithering through the water as his feet sank a little deeper; he curled up his toes inside his shoes then felt rooted there, a part of this place forever.

"Hold it, Billy." The rope stopped moving. Reilly heard Billy Wayne cough something up, heard it hit the water with a heaviness he knew it shouldn't have.

"She's on the far right side of it. We gotta wait for her to go to the middle or she'll flop out when it breaks water. Let her back down slow, Billy."

"Yessir."

Reilly pulled his feet out of the water still holding the hook in front of him. He turned and walked fast up the embankment, a chill spreading down his neck to the center of his back. He walked in the direction of the beer bag then dropped the gaff and sat cross-legged on the ground, waited for the light.

"Just let her hang, BW."

"There enough slack?"

"Hell yeah, she's hit bottom already."

The light bounced in Reilly's face as they came up toward him. "I thought you'd have us a full fire goin' by now, yank." Red Willie shined the light ahead of them while Billy Wayne and Reilly gathered dry sticks and brush from the woods. They came back and dropped an armful each into a pile. Red Willie squatted and struck a match to the brown pine needles beneath it, then struck three more and dropped them burning in the bottom of the brush. Reilly got down on his hands and knees and blew hard until the pine needles glowed and the brush and small sticks began to catch fire. He stood up and Billy Wayne handed him a beer out of the burlap sack; Reilly passed it to Red Willie then reached in and got one for himself.

"She's a big one all right," Red said, popping open his beer.

"How can you tell?"

"You pull on that rope and you can tell, Cap."

"Nope. I knew she was big as soon as we got to the creek. Yank, perk your nose up a bit, what do you smell?"

Reilly sniffed. "Burning wood."

"Well that's the difference between you and me, son."

"I smelled it, Red," Billy Wayne said just before he raised the can of beer to his mouth and slurped loudly.

"Dead fish, yank."

"Yeah?"

"The stronger the smell the bigger the turtle, son."

"What do you mean?"

"These things eat fish and frogs mainly, but their gullet ain't big enough to swallow 'em whole so they end up takin' chunks out of things as they pass by. A man smells a lot of carcass in a water hole, he knows somethin's feedin'."

"I don't smell anything like that."

"That's 'cause you ain't got the nose for it, yank. Them fish float downstream but if you got a nose for things like me and BW here, well then you can still smell it in the air, see."

Reilly took a long swallow from his beer and imagined a turtle that took chunks out of things, its head popping out of its shell open-mouthed then chomping down and tearing free with a quick twist of its leathery neck. "Why doesn't it just swim away from the net?"

"Hell, you know why from the little ones we caught, Cap."

"The net helps her get fish, yank. She'll come up for air then go right back down to her feedin' place. Then we pull on the bottom rope to feel where she is. When she's in the middle, then shit, that's all she wrote." Red Willie took a pint-sized bottle out of one of his overall pockets, opened it, and took a long pull.

"Ooo, I'll have some of that."

Red passed the bottle to Billy Wayne. He swallowed then chased it with his beer. "Cap?"

Reilly took it from Billy, swallowed once then held himself tight against the cough, the first layer of skin on his tongue and throat feeling fresh killed; he passed the bottle back to Billy Wayne and swallowed cool beer fast.

"You divorce that Texas gal yet?"

"Shit," Billy said.

"Boy, she did a number on you. Even my Martha, God bless her, wouldn't a gone that far."

"That's because Jude is a class A, number one, ball breakin' bitch, boys, and I'll tell ya somethin' right now, the good Lord give me the opportunity to see that through the time I done in Rapides Parish."

"Shit, if that's God's way feel free to count me out, son."

"Yeah but I'm talkin' different, Red, them bars give a man some time with hisself; hell I ain't even 'sposed to be drinkin'. I got to report down to that center to piss in a jar for 'em whenever they call me for it."

"Don't tell me no sad stories, friend. I killed a damn truckload of Germans for Uncle Sam and I ain't seen a disability check in fourteen fuckin' years."

Reilly looked at Billy Wayne standing in the firelight, saw how lean and sunken his face had gotten in the last year, a harbor for shadows. "How long were you in there, Billy?"

Billy Wayne took another drink from the bottle then chased it again with his beer. "Eight months and sixteen days."

Reilly looked away and into the fire, felt his face muscles go slack as he went into a stare, his eyes open and nonblinking even as they began to water from the smoke; he looked deep into it at the glowing coals beneath the unburnt wood, saw them breathing with their own heat, thought how nice it would be to be able to wade through them, to lie down in them without burning. He watched a small blue flame in its center weaving back and forth, licking up at some brush, and he remembered the cobra he'd seen with Mimi.

Her roommate was gone and they had spent all morning and part of the afternoon in bed, the clock radio stuck on a soft-rock FM station; they had made love for hours, had held each other tight until their arms slipped from their backs with the sweat, until the room was humid with their smells. Then they showered and dressed and went out into the cold Sunday afternoon to find bagels and coffee, ended up at The Animal Reserve.

They were looking at the reptiles and he had tapped the glass after reading the sign that said not to. The snake uncoiled fast and rose up out of itself, its head fanning to twice its normal size, and Mimi had pulled him back as the top part of it began to weave from side to side, slow and controlled, then shot itself straight forward into the glass making a knocking sound that made them both jump.

Reilly closed his eyes against the smoke and tried to see her face. He saw her eyes then her hair in the sunlight. He thought harder and saw her mouth and nose but this time he didn't see her forehead or cheeks. But he had her smell and her taste. Sometimes he'd be working in the garden with his grandfather, holding a half-full basket in each hand while the white-bearded old man stooped over between the vegetable rows, a V of sweat sticking his faded workshirt to his back; he would half straighten up, then without looking hold the okra or green beans or tomatoes out for Reilly to put a basket under. Her smell came to him at these times. Among all the other earth smells his mind would play tricks on him; he'd be handling tomatoes when his nose would be filled with the milky scent of her cheek and throat, or he'd be rinsing the vegetables with the hose at the gate, letting cool well water run over his dirty hands, and then he'd taste her, would all of a sudden know in his mouth the salty sweetness of her down there. He would keep doing what he was doing, wouldn't think about it, but it always left something opened in him, something drafty and unfinished. But he could never see her whole face, just fragments of it, and he knew that when he could see all of her in his head talking and laughing or quiet and watching, that he would be very close to not needing her anymore, that her place inside him would fill up with something else.

Reilly opened his eyes and looked back into the fire. He heard the Louisiana twang in both men's talking and felt he couldn't be farther away from her if he tried. He drank from his beer then lowered it quickly; he knew what it had been doing, that it hadn't been helping but was instead making liquid and fertile all those feelings he was trying to dry up, was pulling him inside himself to a hollow place full of bad echoes, and he knew if he had the keys to Billy's truck he'd be running through the woods right now, would get in and start it up, would drive to Le Mae's and fill up the tank, buy two large coffees to go then get on the interstate north. In two days he'd be with her, his face buried in her curly blond hair, smelling it, kissing her neck, not knowing what to say, hoping she'd say it for him, would be shocked at what he had done to see her and just hold him tight, invite him back.

"Yank, you gone deaf or is this liquor a bit much for your constitution?"

"Hell no." Reilly cleared his throat.

"Then let's go, Cap." Billy Wayne turned his back on the fire and walked unsteadily toward the creek. Reilly followed after him but Red stopped him with his arm. He gripped Reilly's shoulder with his thick-fingered hand and looked him in the eye. "We're going to pull her. Now you're goin' to have to wade in about waist deep to do any good here tonight."

Reilly was looking back into Red's face lit up gold from the fire; he saw how crooked his nose was, how the skin hung dry and loose over the sharp bones of his face, a few days' growth of white and gray whiskers covering most of it; his eyes were locked into the old man's and he felt their hardness even though he knew that Red Willie liked him, that he called him yank with a tease in his voice Reilly understood. "Yeah, no problem, Red."

Red handed him the gaff. "Just hook her in the head hole of the shell and pull her back to the beach." He was mimicking a pulling movement with both his bare arms.

"Yeah, no problem."

"How 'bout some light down here!"

Red pulled his flashlight out of his overall pocket and flicked it on. Reilly walked ahead of him and saw his shadow on the ground, then the sand and slow-moving muddy water.

Red stood beside him and shined the light in the direction of the cork.

Reilly couldn't see it.

"She's layin' right smack in the middle."

Reilly leaned forward and saw where the two lines came into the water at a steep angle from each bank, were pulled tight and unmoving in the current.

"God damn!" Billy Wayne shouted from up the embankment behind them.

"All right," Red said, "when you hear that cork pop up you gotta figure you have another half a minute before she breaks water. When she does, let out a holler and one of us'll be down with the light."

"Just leave it here with me."

"No sir, you need both hands for what you got to do, so just give us a call, yank. Now get in that creek and catch us a loggerhead." Red Willie turned with the light and walked up the embankment to the hickory tree, rope, and Billy Wayne.

Reilly's bladder was full but he didn't want to call out to them to wait for him. He pulled the gaff back until he could touch the hook then turned it with its point facing down.

"Ready, Cap?"

"*No,* let me get in there first."

"There ain't no guarantee she'll stay in that net, yank!"

Reilly walked forward in the sand until he could feel the water moving against his ankles. He stopped and took a deep breath, opened his eyes wide and looked straight ahead and to his left. He couldn't see the net lines; he wanted to urinate, to get out of that warm water he couldn't see and go sit by the fire, sit by the fire with Mimi, the two of them here together, alone.

"Let's do her," Reilly heard Red say. He heard the rope rising out of the water to his right then whizzing over the hickory branch. It stopped. "Shit," Billy Wayne said. It moved again then stopped, moved then stopped, and Reilly knew only one of them was pulling. He gripped the gaff so hard it felt like a part of his arms. He rushed forward into the water to his knees then to his mid-thigh. He stepped forward again then pulled back as his foot touched something hard. His heart was beating fast in his chest and head and ears. He took a deep breath and stepped well over the hard thing. The current was stronger now, pushing at his hip; he was conscious of his crotch being underwater and he wished for the light. "Hey! Are you both pulling? 'Cause if it's only one of you, how about some light?"

The rope stopped. "Billy's got a problem, yank." It started up again and Reilly listened to what he had been hearing, heard Billy Wayne's coughing turn into a heave and retch, heard the gush-splash of his insides as it hit the ground; then he heard the thrashing out there ahead of him in the dark.

"Shit, Red, light!"

The rope kept moving then stopped. "Has the cork popped yet?"

"No! Something alive!"

"I'm tyin' her now!"

Reilly spaced his feet apart in the creek's bottom then lowered the hook end of the gaff in the water ahead of him and pulled back his arms to feel it. This is it, he thought. This is the kill. And he heard a sound he had never before heard but right away recognized it for what it was. "Bring the goddamned light, Red!"

"I'm right behind ya, yank."

Reilly saw the light jerking ahead of him on the water then higher to the opposite bank, to the bare roots of trees half in the creek, half in the earth, their surfaces smooth from the water, hanging curved and rigid like the dead legs of a spider. "Fucking snake caves," Reilly said and began to run in place against the current, his heart beating so fast he could feel it in his throat. He heard Red Willie stop at the edge of the creek then saw the light steady as it moved away from the bank then over him to his left, to that sound.

"Holy shit."

"Get in there and snag the shit out of her, boy!"

Reilly didn't go forward. He looked down the gaff at what was moving awkward and heavy in the net in front of him. His eyes fixed on the shell first; it was bigger than the round aluminum skiffs he and Joey used to slide down Nettle Hill in; it was smooth and so dark green it was almost black. Then he looked at what was making that sound, a thick fleshy claw that stretched five or six inches out of one of the leg holes then flapped back against the shell with a power that made Reilly move his legs faster.

"Well go on, boy!" Red was laughing.

"Shine it near its head!"

The light moved up to where the cork was and Reilly saw it, the size of a small boy's fist, sticking three or four inches out of the shell, a double ridge of barnaclelike bumps along the top of it with a black beak that was opening then snapping shut, a tiny eye shining gold in the light. "It's got a head like a fucking vulture!"

"Snag her, yank!" Red wasn't laughing anymore.

Reilly gripped the gaff then lunged it out at the turtle; it hit the center of its shell with a crack that traveled up through the gaff into Reilly's hands; he jumped back, wanting to throw it away from him, feeling like he'd just reached under the shell and touched it with his bare hands.

"Get in closer, boy!"

Reilly stepped forward a half step, the current pushing against his legs, hips, and buttocks. He began to move in deeper. He felt the weight of the gaff in his hands. This is eight feet long, he thought, that's as close as I have to get. Then he heard the water splashing behind him and spun around quick to see the silhouette of Billy Wayne against Red's light, small-shouldered and thin-necked, his ears sticking out from his head. "Shit!" Reilly said.

"C'mon, boys!" Red shouted.

Billy Wayne came and stood waist deep in the water beside Reilly. "You hook her, Cap. We'll pull her together, by God."

He was breathing loud and it sounded to Reilly like it was coming from someplace wet inside his chest, and the air smelled sour around him.

"Okay." Reilly stepped closer to the net and felt his lower belly wetten. He couldn't see the head and the claw had stopped moving.

"She's pulled in, smart old bitch," Billy Wayne said. He leaned into Reilly a bit with his shoulder, but Reilly didn't move. He breathed deep and reached the hook of the gaff toward the head hole of the shell.

"That's it, yank!"

He rested the gaff against the net then pushed over it to the front. He lined up the hook, turned it so it was pointing at the hole, then with both his arms he swung into it and pulled to him, his back and arms straining with the weight. The big shell turned with his pull, the hole facing them, and Reilly looked straight ahead into it and saw the reflection of Red's light in both its tiny eyes just before they closed.

"Keep her movin' once she's off that net, now!"

"Ready, Cap?"

"Yeah."

They pulled hard backing up in the water with long slow steps, the current moving against the sides of their legs, and Reilly felt the weight of it as it slid off the net into the water. He stepped on the hard thing again then jumped over it. "Easy, Cap." They pulled the gaff ahead of them and lifted their legs higher as they got closer to the bank and Red Willie's light. Billy Wayne let go when their legs got free of the water and Reilly pulled her the rest of the way to where Red was standing.

"Keep her movin', yank! Get her away from the creek."

Reilly pulled and felt the drag of it as it moved through the sand; he was breathing hard and as he started up the embankment, his legs and arms burning, he gripped the gaff tighter and pulled the turtle to the flat ground near the fire. He turned around and dropped the gaff then straightened up and breathed deep through his nose as Red Willie and Billy Wayne came up with the light.

"God damn," Billy Wayne almost whispered through his breathing. He squatted and rested his elbows on his knees, put his head down.

The fire was burning brighter now and Red Willie turned off the flashlight and dropped it into his pocket. He walked over and stood beside the turtle. "Man, ain't she majestic. Look at her, yank. She's old enough to be your gran'mammy."

Reilly looked down at it; its claws were out now resting on the ground, its head still pulled in the hole at the front of its huge shell.

"God damn," Billy said.

Reilly could smell him over the smoke of the fire, could smell the half-burned whiskey in his sweat, the sweet and sour of his insides in the air.

"Now yank, you got to respect a reptile like this." Red walked spread-legged until the turtle was beneath him then straddled it, sat on the highest part, his bare feet kept well away from the claws on each side. He ran his hand over the light circular patterns of its shell. "She's a beauty. Man, she's royalty." He reached into his overalls pocket and pulled out the pint bottle and opened it, took a quick sip, then wiped his mouth with his bare arm and held it out to Billy Wayne.

Billy raised his head and took it.

Red looked up at Reilly, smiling. "Did she feel like a five pounder to you, yank?"

"No, sir."

"That's right, son, that's right."

Billy Wayne stood up fast and coughed hard into his hand then wiped it on his pants and spit out into the darkness toward the creek. He held the bottle out to Reilly.

"No thanks."

Red Willie nodded his head at the fire. "Yank, get me somethin' burnin' outta there."

Reilly bent down and pulled out a short hickory stick, one end smoking and glowing bright orange.

"Just right," Red said. "Now yank, these things don't live as long as they do by bein' nice to everybody all the time. But when you kill one you want to do it quick like; you don't want to give it no pain." Red reached down into one of the deep pockets in his pant leg and pulled out a knife, its blade long and gray.

Reilly squatted down near the fire, his pants wet and heavy, and looked over at Billy Wayne. He was standing, his arms hanging limp at his sides, the bottle empty at his feet; he was looking down at Red Willie sitting on that big shell. His mouth was half open and his eyes were fixed in a stare, but he looked to Reilly like he was sleeping, sleeping awake and standing up, turning himself in and away from the place his forty years had taken him, and Reilly thought of Jude, could see her expression as she grabbed the hot iron skillet off the stove, a potholder between the black handle and her gripping hands, as she swung it at Billy Wayne, her sad face contorting even tighter with "You bastard!," the side of the pan spinning then catching Billy Wayne square in the mouth. Then Jude's face began to turn into Mimi's and Reilly stood up, focused himself on what the old man was saying.

"Now the meanness that has kept this old turtle alive is the same meanness we're goin' to use to kill her. Watch what she does, yank." Red held the glowing stick in his left hand, the knife in his right, its cutting edge facing up. He lowered the stick until its orange tip was right in front of the head hole. He paused then pushed it in, held it, then pulled it out quick. "Now she's hurt and pissed off," Red Willie said without looking up. He lowered the stick again and held it in front of the hole then began to move it slow back and forth like a bow over a fiddle.

Reilly looked into the hole from where he was; he wanted to see its eyes again before it died and he thought of what the turtle must be seeing from inside its house, smoking orange then gray wood, smoking orange then gray.

Red pulled the stick to within an inch of the shell then out it came, its black beak snapping loud onto the burning end of the stick; Red pulled it forward and the turtle's head followed, stretched out of the hole until Reilly could see the bumpy flesh of its neck pull smooth. He heard the stick crack just as Red Willie brought the knife down under the throat and pulled toward him and to his right, his left arm jerking up as the base of the neck snapped back into the hole like rubber, the turtle's head still connected to the smoking hickory stick above Red Willie. Blood was pumping out of the hole in short quick spurts and Reilly looked at the head, at its little eyes closed tight, at the loose flap of neck that was dripping blood down onto Red's arm and shoulder.

"She didn't feel a thing, yank, not a thing." Red stood up and walked through the blood that was coming slower now from the hole, was turning into a trickle. He held the stick out to Reilly.

"No thank you."

Red smiled then stopped and looked down at the head, inspecting it for a moment like he would a splinter in a small child's finger. He dropped it into the fire.

"Let's have the knife, Red," Billy Wayne said loud and hoarse behind them.

Red Willie handed him the wet blade handle-first. Billy took it then held it between his teeth as he bent over and with a groan pulled and turned the shell upside down, its pale yellow bottom facing the sky, the turtle's claws hanging out of the holes. He took the knife in his hand and worked quickly, pushing its point between the light-colored plates of the bottom and where the shell becomes dark; he pulled toward him and with a dry ripping sound cut and tore all the way around the shell. Then he pulled it out and pressed the tip of the blade below the head hole and moved it straight down the center of the plate, never pushing more than an inch or so until he got to the end of the shell. He dropped the knife then pried the dissected bottom up from the claw holes and pulled it up, flesh and gristle sticking to it; Billy Wayne picked up the knife again and cut through until he could pull the half piece free and toss it behind him.

"That's it, Billy. You're doin' all the good, friend, you're doin' all the good."

Billy Wayne cut free the other half of the plate, threw it over his shoulder without looking, then began to work around the flat mass of entrails that Reilly was now looking down at, standing over Billy Wayne and the dead turtle.

Red Willie leaned over to him. "Pay attention, son, there's somethin' here you oughta see."

Reilly backed away a step to make room for more light from the fire. He listened to Billy Wayne's heavy breathing and occasional grunting, watched him working away with the knife under the pale organs that gleamed now in the firelight, that was giving off a smell stronger than Billy's, a hot smell, almost sweet, and

Reilly was struck by it; he couldn't smell anything else and it suddenly occurred to him that he was smelling more than just the guts of an old turtle, and he knew what it was, that if secrets have a smell, this is it.

"They're unconnected now," Billy Wayne said. "Stand back, Cap."

Reilly and Red Willie stepped away from the shell as Billy Wayne got around one side and pulled it up then held it for a moment as the entrails began to slide out of it onto the ground in front of the fire. He raised it a bit higher and Reilly watched as they sloshed out in a neat shiny heap onto the dirt. "Show him, Red."

Reilly looked at Billy Wayne then at Red Willie.

"See it?" the old man asked, looking from Reilly to the ground then back again.

Reilly looked down at the entrails, saw big and small pieces; some were light-colored, others were dark, almost red, and they all seemed to fit together perfectly even as they lay now in the dirt, cut away from the body they had been part of for years. Then he saw the movement in the middle, saw one of the small parts there twitching. He bent over and looked closer. "Jesus Christ."

"How do you like that, yank?"

"I can't believe it."

"It's somethin' ain't it, Cap?"

Reilly was squatting now and could hear it too, a soft flapping against two bigger parts, its small dark mass jerking at a controlled and regular pace, not twitching Reilly could see, but beating.

"We timed one at sixteen minutes once, Cap."

Reilly looked up at the two men; they were standing close

together, looking down at him, Billy Wayne's face yellow and beaded with a bad-smelling sweat, the white whiskers of Red Willie's face almost glowing with the light from the fire, and for a second Reilly felt he was in the presence of two very wise and friendly ghosts. "I don't understand it."

"I've only seen it in the *old* loggerheads, yank. I've kilt young-uns, but I've only seen this in the old ones."

They both looked down again at the turtle's heart, still beating slow and calm, the only movement in the pile of entrails.

"I call it the last dance, yank."

Reilly was shaking his head. He heard Billy Wayne working again behind them, scraping the shell of its meat. He felt the fire on his face, the tickle of a sweat drop as it rolled down off his nose into the pile, and he caught the soiled leather smell of Red Willie, looked at the old man's face watching the heart, his hard blue eyes softened now, the fire's flames flickering in the wetness of them, and they held a gaze that Reilly recognized, that gave his face the look that comes to faces whenever they restudy a thing that exposes a truth they have already come to know very well, a look both respectful and resigned, and Reilly knew where he had seen it before; on Billy Wayne, when he would talk about Jude or jail and his drinking, and on his grandfather's face too, when he would have to reach for the cane leaning against the fence of the garden after less than an hour's work, his shoulders slumped and tired-looking. And on Jude, when she would light a cigarette with her coffee and silently watch her husband. Red Willie's eyes moved to Reilly's. "You'll have a good amount of meat to give your gran'-maw, yank."

"Yeah." Reilly stood up. "Yeah, that's right." He didn't feel like he was outside anymore; he needed air. He looked behind at

Billy Wayne and watched as he dropped big pieces of dark flesh into Red's sack, then he turned away from the fire and Red Willie and the heart he believed must still be beating and walked toward the creek, his body cooling slightly as he moved into the darkness.

"We'll get the net in the mornin', yank."

"I gotta piss." He walked down the embankment and over the sand and heard the black water moving by in front of him. He peed into it, looked straight ahead into the night and saw himself getting out of Billy's truck after having already dropped Red off, having watched him in the headlights' glare walk barefoot through the beer cans, his gaff over one shoulder, a portion of turtle meat wrapped in a piece of burlap under his arm; then they would be at his grandparents' place and Billy would squeeze his shoulder, would say, "G'night, Cap. My love to your gran'maw." He would close the door softly then take his share of turtle meat inside and put it someplace cold, would wash up, then climb into the top bunk and lie still in the cool wind of the electric fan, would breathe deep through his nose and wait for sleep. And as Reilly stood so close to the water that he heard but could not see, something popping in the fire behind him, the tired voices of Billy Wayne and Red Willie hanging in the air as they finished their work, he felt himself become part of the darkness, part of the sand and creek and hickory trees, part of whatever was living out there around him, and in his solitude there he felt again the coolness of the hollow place inside him that still belonged to Mimi, but it was different now, and as he rolled his head until his neck cracked, his body let him know that the place had lost some of its pull, that it had merged with other things inside him.

He turned quickly and walked back up the embankment to the fire, to where the two men were squatting over the entrails, looking from the pile to Billy's watch then back again. He walked over and squatted too, saw the softened eyes of Red Willie, caught the final smell of Billy Wayne. He looked down and waited with them, waited for the end of the soft flapping sound the dark piece was making, jerking slow and controlled against two bigger parts.

ALSO BY ANDRE DUBUS III

BLUESMAN

In the summer of 1967, Leo Suther has one more year of high
school to finish and a lot more to learn. He's in love with the
beautiful Allie Donovan who introduces him to her father,
Chick—a construction foreman and avowed Communist. Soon
Leo finds himself in the midst of a consuming love affair and an
intense testing of his political values. Chick's passionate views
challenge Leo's perspective on the escalating Vietnam conflict
and on just where he stands in relation to the new people in his
life. Throughout his—and the nation's—unforgettable "summer
of love," Leo is learning the language of the blues, which seem to
speak to the mourning he feels for his dead mother, his occasion-
ally distant father, and the youth which is fast giving way to
manhood.

Fiction/Literature/0-375-72516-4

HOUSE OF SAND AND FOG

Colonel Behrani, once a wealthy man in Iran, is now a struggling
immigrant willing to bet everything he has to restore his family's
dignity. Kathy Nicolo is a recovering alcoholic and addict whose
house is all she has left, and who refuses to let her hard-won sta-
bility slip away from her. Sheriff Lester Burdon, a married man
who finds himself falling in love with Kathy, becomes obsessed
with helping her fight for justice. Drawn by their competing
desires to the same small house in the California hills and what it
represents to each of them, the three converge on an explosive col-
lision course. This highly acclaimed novel combines unadorned
realism with profound empathy to create a devastating explo-
ration of the American Dream gone awry.

Fiction/Literature/0-375-72734-5

VINTAGE CONTEMPORARIES
Available at your local bookstore, or call toll-free to order:
1-800-793-2665 (credit cards only).